William Ottoway's Utopia
and
other stories

May Saman favour reconciliation over revenge !

Christopher Griffith

Chris G

William Ottoway's Utopia and other stories

© Christopher Griffith 2019

Contents

INTRODUCTION

Each of these five stories started life as full-length novels, though in course of their completion I was also at work on scripts, stage plays and a considerable body of poetry. As I wrote over the years, I tried hard to concentrate on one discipline but I was unable to commit to any single form, the realization slowly dawning on me that the most effective way to proceed might be to merge them together. The result is this offering – each piece novel in conception, poetic by birth, scripted and staged throughout their short life, with a hint of non-fiction too…

William Ottoway's Utopia concerns the dream of a man who seeks to escape stresses of everyday life for promised ease in this world's tropics; to his dismay, he is unable to flee influence of the one appliance which has arguably shaped all our experience in the last half century, the humble television set! William is a good man, but will he be ravaged and ruined by his brother Tom who brings discord and disharmony to his island paradise?

Rick With A (Bipolar) View details the experience of a young man suffering from bipolar disorder who wants to be a professional DJ. Unsure whether or not the repetitive beats of electronic music and his obsession with trance and techno may be the cause of his illness, he nevertheless accepts offer of a Friday night gig and takes the roof off the nightclub, coming down back at home in glow and reflection of his achievement.

If all this sounds too intense then do please head over to *Break Out the Bubbly!!,* a comic piece set in a supermarket whose Manager is acting in very strange manner indeed. The initial boredom felt by our hero Emily is quickly shattered by Carol's arrival and subsequent farce as she seems intent on closing the shop during opening hours to conduct inquisitions in the boardroom! The champagne keeps going missing, you see, and she needs to find the culprit. Is he, or she, a little closer to home than everyone thinks?

Fantasy for the next story, *Saman's Revenge*, in which our titular hero is seriously miffed with the Earth-goddess Thera; she's punished him an aeon ago for misdemeanour which he firmly believes really wasn't his fault at all. Anyway, when you're immortal and old as the hills themselves it doesn't bother you too much to wait a few millennia before exacting your revenge on modern day teenagers Jack, Roxie, her boyfriend Mark and his brother Norman. But what is the young people's relation to Thera, and temple ruins on top of the village hill, Shadyridge?

Which leaves *Young Shakespeare*, my imaginative retelling of some of Will's 'lost years' when he reached London; after all, who wouldn't want to fall in love with Anne, listen in awe to Sir Walter Raleigh's perorations on, well who knows, meet his future friend and rival Christopher 'Kit' Marlowe, then cogitate at length upon the Reformation against whose profound change the budding writer begins to conclude he might wish to work?

I do hope you find a piece, or more, amongst the five which appeals to you – like all authors, I take very seriously the reader-writer bond and agreement. You are kind enough to give of your time to read my work, and I would be overjoyed if I knew that your experience in doing so might have been one you deemed worthwhile; I am married to my lovely wife with our toddler son and almost fourteen years old black cat who's starting to get a bit slow about the place, although she did enjoy proofreading these stories!

WILLIAM OTTOWAY'S UTOPIA

1

A still.
The Earth.
Stunning blue-green admixture belying division inherent in ruling species its territories.
The image lessens in size.
We are drawing back, out that the picture which moments before seemed real now shown to be fraudulent, framed by parameters of a vast television set.
This is High Screen.
Its authority absolute.
Its influence profound.
Its demands incessant.
Before it, clearing, habitation occupied by smaller television screens.
One.
Ten.
No, a hundred.
Each running subject material obscene, perversion violating taboos honoured by generations previous.
And there, look there, people (Utopians).
In positions of worship.
Under obeisance to all didactic that flows from the screens.
And still we draw further back from habitation.
Through jungle.
Over clifftop.
To beach and then sea.
That it stretches like azure carpet, unruffled by turbulence of tide, blue sky bending back to horizon where a mass of islands studs the water, forming giant archipelago.
Small ship upon the sea, to which we now draw.
Narrowing, focusing upon its captain tending rigging at bow.
Sudden scream from below decks brings him there.

He bursts into a cabin.
Andrew, his voyager, writhes around, fighting the air above him.
Captain pinions his arms.
'Wake up! Wake up!'
Andrew's eyes shoot open, his stare vehement.
'He is coming. His brother is here.'
Crewmen fill the doorway behind, crossing themselves vigorously.
'Get out!' yells the Captain. 'You must leave my vessel.'
'Have we far to go?'
Cry sounds from above decks.
'What now?'

Climbs to the bow.
'What is it? What's wrong?'
Captain takes binoculars from crewman and puts them to his eyes.
Andrew strains, but can see, a figure swimming off to starboard.
'He's in no distress.'
'But for the sharks. Intercept him.'
Shout from the stern now.
Crewmen haul a body up and over the side there.
The man is shark-bitten but alive.
Taken below for attendance.
Andrew follows.

Sits.
Studies the injured.
Gaunt and bedraggled.
Piercing blue eyes on a sudden boring into Andrew's very soul.
The man grips him with bony hand.
'Thank you. Thank you for coming.'
'Who is he, swimming out to sea?'
Low moan escapes him.
'Your brother?'
Captain bursts in, pulls open the curtain covering the cabin's porthole.
'Utopia.'
Blue-white waves spill onto glittering beaches, canopy of emerald leaves spread over trees running round edge of endless sand.

Ship's anchor is weighed.
Small rowing boat lowered for Andrew.
'You have one hour. We set sail then.'

Andrew rows, heckles rising on his neck as he nears land.
Runs boat aground.
Enters first break in trees.
Rough track leading away into the forest.
Sun's rays slant gracefully.
Natural peace broken only by melodious chirrup of birds.
Object lying half-hidden in the grass.
Andrew uncovers an antique television.
Blocky screen.
Buttons marked one to eight running down its side.
He notices footprints.
Follows them.
Small clearings.
Streams.
Signs of order.
A larger clearing.
Habitation evident.
Television screens littering its landscape.
All showing identical motion picture.
Point of light explodes.
Expands.
Contracts.
Expires.
Explodes.
Expands.
Contracts.
Expires.
At prominence, High Screen shows still.
Image transcendent.
Man's gradual rise from ape heritage.
Utopians are kneeling before it in homage.
Swaying gently.
Arms aloft in worship.
One notices Andrew.
Rage contorts her features.

'The blasphemer! The blasphemer is come!'
Clearing irrupts into life.
They give chase.
Andrew races back through the jungle.

Emerges on beach.
To boat.
Rows frantically out to sea.
Utopians flood into the water after him.
Desperately claw at the sides of his vessel.
He clatters the oars against them.
Somehow, he is free.
Chase, though, is given still.
Andrew yells at the Captain.
Ship turned.
He is hauled up the side.
Utopians clamber thereon.
Repelled by crew.
Boat moves away.
Scream from below decks.
'You tend him.'

Andrew rushes to the cabin.
The rescued is apoplectic.
'Manou! You can't leave him. They'll tear him to pieces.'
Captain appears in doorway.
'I'm sure they already have.'
The fellow beckons Andrew towards him.
Bids turn him over.
Great whip marks streak his back.
Terrible, deep red gashes lacerate the skin.
'How do you come by them?
'He who you see in your sleep. I had to reveal my mind.'
'Why me?'
'Subliminal messaging helps us care for one another. It is meant to unify.'
'Why me, though?'
'You sought community. My Utopia.'
'Tell me of it.'

Boat steams on.
Circumnavigating, not leaving the island behind.

2

School dormitory.
Henry approaches his friend, William.
The latter, in bed, concentrating on the book he is reading.
'And what are you studying tonight, my dear Ottoway?'
'Milton's *Paradise Lost*.'
'How goes it with man?'
'Not good, I'm afraid. His temptation was too great to resist.'
'I wonder what the apple of our age will prove to be, William.'
'Money, I fear.'
'Yet our progenitors were not expelled for accruing wealth, but for acquiring knowledge beyond that afforded their ken.'
'They were tricked to it though.'
'For sure, but the admonition stood beforehand. They listened to the wrong god.'
'I don't understand.'
'Nor I really. But the world stands testament to their tomfoolery nonetheless. I know, let's make it better.'
'How ever might we manage that?'
'The flaming sword prevented Adam and Eve from regaining paradise. No such cherub stands in our way. Come to mine at the weekend and we'll work out the finer details.'

Henry's home.
William is finishing dinner with Henry and Henry's parents.
'Well that's enough talk about school. Come, what do you boys plan to achieve at semester break?'
'We are going to make the world perfect, father.'
'Well, we are going to try to improve upon it anyway.'
'And how are you planning to achieve such, goal?'
'By abandoning money.'
'And God.'
'Two firm bedrocks of civilization. Do you think their absence will be missed?'
'God is gone anyway, father.'
'Leaving this other to support man's famed frugality. What do you

make of the boys' plans, Agatha?'

'How will you convert them into practice?'

'It will be easy. Who wouldn't want to live in a better world?'

'All of us, presently.'

'All of us?'

'We have been conditioned so. You, from birth, so that you are of it unaware. But we, well there is no excuse for our capitulation. We knew the world well before we surrendered it.

'To what, madam?'

'Myopia, William, and of that its most foolish incarnation – mankind's asseveration that he can go it alone, without guidance, without protection.'

'Protection? Modernity has freed us from every danger which threatened yesteryear's generations. Democracy, liberalism, secularism, progression, we have never known such safety, and in such numbers, across so much of the world.'

'The ideals, in themselves, are of virtue. But they have been hijacked.'

'By whom?'

'The vainglorious. Hypocrites, in the main, who basking in perceived shortcomings of opponents miss entirely their own deficiency of conception concerning the same matter.'

'But of whom do you speak?'

'The great sages of recent, and now present, history. Men, mostly, whose drive to prove others wrong, and that through contumely, only exacerbates their own abject error of self-ignorance.'

'I have never met such.'

'Yet they are the very pillars of our age. Sophists, and dissemblers, who gladly dismantle truth, thus pushing it further from all our understanding.'

'But truth is relative, surely? And the ideals too, of which I have made mention, part of new order, a new reality even?'

'Certainly, yet one for which they, by their infection, have wholly unprepared any of us, instead leaving the race so bare to the elements that in our collective delusion and self-absorption, fostered by their lead, we are unleashing the very evils we consider through our brave and bold endeavor to be nullifying. In search for a better world.'

'But evil is none such. I mean, it is element of the past, banished by scientific advance.'

'Banished, but not destroyed. Displaced, dear boy, only.'

'But this is preposterous. We are far in advance of such superstition. Science has dispensed with all figment of ancient imagination, and I say again it has vanquished such fancy. That is why we live so happily now.'

'Then why do you, product of such contentment, seek escape from it?'

'I don't know.'

'And why under such super abundance of liberty, does mental turmoil among us gain with such rapidity?'

'I'm not sure.'

'We have progressed, of course, scientifically but psychologically, in there, where mind, imagination and dream converge, well those unguarded pastures are not yet tended, much less claimed by the good shepherd who has overcome this reality.

'Then what can we do?'

'Dream. But nobly. You must pursue your enterprise. Shine its light example to the world. Hold onto it. Never let it die. That is the difference between happiness and disillusionment. Such is the wisdom of current thought. So go dream.

William dreams he is on Utopia island, wandering listlessly but contentedly.
Suddenly he is at feast with the islanders, dining in joyful mood.
Henry's father, among them, chokes.
Produces, television, from his mouth.
William sits bolt upright, feels his throat.

3

William's house.

He and Henry talk.

Film version of *Lord of the Flies* plays on television to their side.

'It must be in the tropics. A hot climate, conducive to leisure.'

'But I would not wish us indolent.'

'On the contrary, by natural course we shall earn our keep. Catching fish.'

'Plucking fruit.'

'Gathering wood for fire.'

'Warmth, and for cooking in the evening.'

'With wholesome thought that we have left a thoroughly imperfect world behind.'

'Agreed, then. With money, and with God, we shall dispense.'

'Must we really lose God?'

'Your faith is fragile, Henry.'

'Yet still I believe. Very well, no God. Nor shall intoxicants, neither drugs of any kind, remove us from conscious awareness.'

'Smoking banned.'

'Technology outlawed - no computers, nor radio, nor certainly television will be permitted.'

'We shall live quietly.'

'Without distraction.'

'So in peace.'

'Modern morality our standard, our guide. What is it?'

'The world is cold, Henry. Morals are no match for it. Look how it has ensnared my brother.'

'He trapped himself remember, by gambling everyone else's money away. Morality did its best to steady him, William, but he was already leaning before he was felled. Do you have conception of his whereabouts?'

'Only that he is far off, and better I think both for Heather and me that way. I would not want him bringing bad ways upon my sister again. I don't think her nerves would hold.'

'He encouraged her to gamble?'

'No, that is not in her nature. She disapproved, Henry, of his

immorality of thought.'
'Brought on by the habit?'
'No. Thousands flutter without losing their compass. His swung wildly because of his outlook.'
'His unbelief?'
'No, for my sister has ever been plural in her conception.'
'What, then, William?'
'Heather is meticulous. In all that she aims concentration towards, she devotes herself deeply. She has told me often how writing enlarges her understanding, but that it is her reading material for which she retains deepest regard.'
'What has this to do with Tom?'
'Civility of study.'
'You've lost me, Ottoway.'
'She couldn't stand his subversion, intentioned subversion of the holiness he studied. A superficial perusal of the philosophy, she claimed, read scornfully and in consequence through eyes rebellious to its teaching.'
'Come, you can't plug a man's reading matter. And his interpretation thereof is his own.'
'Perhaps we might have helped though, directed him from trouble.'
'Tom brought his own woes upon himself. He kept bad company, and was in consequence corrupted so.'
'But Heather and I, we could have intervened.'
'To be trapped yourselves? No, William, you did right to recede.'
'He is not malign like them though, I know it.
'He has always had it in him.'
'But not to their extent.'
'For sure, my friend, those villains sowed their tares amongst his wheat, but rain is ever sent upon them both. We are free to make choice with our endeavor, that is God's greatest gift.'
On screen, Jack punches Piggy so that his glasses break.
'I have met someone. William, she is mesmeric. She holds party this weekend. You must join us.'
'I would prefer to work on our plan.'
'You can. At Emily's. I'll explain, I promise. It is so exciting.'
'But tell me of her?'
'She is the most beautiful woman I have ever laid eyes upon, loyal to a fault, graciously showering affection upon me whenever we are

together. She is rich too, Ottoway. You will adore her.'

'What paragon of virtue! I shall attend this gathering then, to make acquaintance. Perchance she may offer of her temperance to fortify this plan of ours.'

'She would be delighted, I'm sure.'

4

Emily's mansion.

Henry opens its heavy front door.

'My dear William, how glad I am you have arrived. Come, come and behold our effort.'

Spacious entrance chamber from which lead luxurious rooms.

Henry excitedly leads William towards one.

Large table in midst.

Full scale model upon it.

'Here. Here it is. This is our home. What do you think?'

'It's marvellous, Henry, wonderful really. A great plan.'

'When do you want to go there?'

'I'm sorry?'

'It's a blueprint, Ottoway, we have the real thing. Emily! Emily! She has bought it, an island. Emily! William, this is Emily, my fiancé.'

'You are to be married?'

'On Utopia. Its perfection will mirror our own bliss.'

'But I forget my manners. I'm delighted, Emily. You have really purchased this, paradise?'

'I fear it shall not remain so.'

'Yes, we know, the vicissitudes of life will undoubtedly intrude.'

'Indeed. Henry has told me you will not permit added extras.'

'We wish to live a basic existence.'

'Yet in contemporary world. You negate money. How will you trade?'

'We shall share.'

'You dispense with appliances also.'

'This is our dream, my darling.'

'Though achievable not without my capital. No drugs, I laud, but in this day and age technology must be our boon companion.'

'We have made our decisions, Emily.'

'Very well. I must return to our guests.'

'Why do we call it a dream?'

'Because it is not yet real.'

'It is odd though, isn't it? Why do we seek escape?'

'We flee not. On the contrary, we will stand at the vanguard of progress, breaking through life's conscious boundary.'

'I don't follow.'

'We call it dream because it is a dream, made real.'

'But then it ceases to be dream.'

'Exactly. Don't you see, humankind, we're collapsing the wall, between conscious and subconscious? Dream is the new reality.'

'But it's completely unplumbed. Shadow and fantasy burst from it if not constrained. Such should remain plugged, surely?'

'Its star is in the ascendant, William. We must follow it. To Eden!' Emily enters.

'But that was wrecked by Satan, remember?'

'There is no devil, William, just shadow, and that God's unconscious matter.'

'I do wish you wouldn't talk like that, Henry. You sound like your mother.'

'There are important differences.'

'I see only the same delusion.'

'Suffered collectively by all generations previous? Honestly, we discover a few stars and galaxies outside our own and suddenly the world is our possession. God lies behind it all.'

'Nonsense. The universe began its own enterprise. It has not room enough for deity.'

'May I not believe still?'

'Your credence bears for it no evidence, and besides hard facts negate the influence of any loving hand in our lives.'

'We are comfortable enough.'

'But of those who are not, who struggle, who suffer, often irreparably, what solace can they draw from God's malice towards them?'

'That is their destiny. Not ours.'

'How do you know ill-fortune shall not curse this venture?'

'It will not, for it is not of this world.'

'Yet, again, contemporary to it. If there is such God as you claim, perhaps he should join us to see firsthand what mess he has made of the place. Why do you smile?'

'For he has already done so, spending earthly life with perverse and adulterous generation just as unbelieving as our own.'

'Pish! Deity sits on high, where we have invented and housed them. God and man do not cohabit.'

'On the contrary, my love, through the denarius handed him when He walked among us, God signified His relation to earthly rule. He loves us, and loves the world He has created for us.'

'This is hokum. Intelligent design, much less that benevolent in intent, is rendered wholly impotent by the savagery some folk are fated to endure. *Reductio ad absurdum*, I'm afraid, must be man's eventual conclusion to concept of benign intervention. Shadow I agree with, and unconscious matter, but none of it concerning God.'

'What do you think, William?'

'I cannot follow.'

5

Speedboat carrying William, Henry and Emily cuts through the clear, blue sea.
Scattered islands across the archipelago, beneath perfect, shaded sky.
William closes his eyes.
Hears definite sound.
Joyous, angelic voices singing them across the surf.
Utopia ahead.
Henry plunges into the shallows to bring them to shore.
Chases Emily up the golden sands of the beach.
Carries her back in his arms.
Rest of the day spent swimming and sunbathing.
William plucks fruit.
Henry gathers wood for fire.
They eat.
'My dear friends, Henry and Emily, I give you Utopia.'
'It is perfect.'
'Magical, truly. It is too sublime for words.'
'Then let us celebrate.'
William dances a jig.
'William, how marvellous it is to see you so happy.'
'I feel exuberant. Ebullient, even.'
They settle back to look up into the starry sky.
'Come, let me tell you of our home - the isle is one of a group forming giant ring this stretch of the Pacific. It is one mile long by a half wide, scouted by nearby islanders who have decided for its size not to settle upon it. There are few monkeys, fewer birds, and the most dangerous creature we might ever come across is a snake. No large animals occupy its environs. Bugs, insects live here aplenty but no lions, no tigers, neither panthers, hippos nor elephants. The island is ours. Let us do with it as we will.'

Marriage ceremony.
Henry utters vows.
Manou, the priest, turns to Emily.
'I, Emily, take thee, Henry, to be my wedded husband, to have and

to hold, from this day forward, for better, for worse, for richer, for poorer, in sickness and in health, to love and to cherish, till death do us part, according to God's holy ordinance; and thereto I pledge thee my faith…I pledge myself to you.'

'Only one pledge is required.'

'But I promise two, Manou, double my love and all my life's devotion.'

'Very well. You are man and wife. Now be alone.'

William remains.

'Why did you not settle here, Manou?'

'For it is too small.'

'Was it the snakes?'

'No, William.'

'What, then?'

'I scouted the island myself. On the far side, there is precipice. Two waterfalls come from it, like floods of tears from the eyes of the cliff face.'

'It sounds magical.'

'Behind them lies the Deep. An abyss, Mr. Ottoway, the Netherworld.'

'Come, Manou, this is superstitious clap.'

'I will never go back. Not alone.'

'Then I shall come with you.'

'You must be asleep.'

'What?'

'Asleep, and in dream.'

'You were dreaming?'

'Conscious effort made awake to meet and join in slumber.'

'You know how to do that?'

'But it is precarious, for the subconscious is unbounded, and unpatrolled. The mind is an open back door, susceptible to influence, both beneficent and amoral.'

'You are paranoid. No one seeks to control the unconscious. We think for ourselves.'

'We think through technology, William. It owns direct access to the mind, whose depths limitless make the universe itself seem infinitesimally small by comparison.

'But you talk fiction, surely? The cosmos is endless, nothing is of greater size.'

'Yet darts thrown against its boundary may still be repelled. A javelin fired into the recesses of the subconscious though, that continues indefinitely.

'To where, the Netherworld? This is too much. We share not thought nor conception with yesterday, let alone that of bygone era.

'Yet the demon possessed of biblical times who cut themselves with stones live on in the minds of those who self-harm today. Our language, and conception changes, but mankind's actions, in the face of evil, remain the same.'

'You speak of technology, though. We have none here.'

'It will come.'

'It shall not.'

'It shall spill, William, like sand through a keyhole.'

'What do you advise then?'

'I have said. Through conscious effort, join in slumber. Tomorrow you have new arrivals. Link minds with those current. Strengthen yourselves for the test ahead.'

Utopians sleep.
In their reverie, Emily lies close to death.
Upon the sandy beach.
Crying out for that denied her.
The ancestral television wedged in the forest pathway.
William starts.

6

Daybreak.
Boat with western voyagers arrives.
Last to disembark, William's own brother, Tom.
William flinches.
Tom, shouldering large bag, hugs him tightly.
'How wonderful it is to see you, William. Henry, how are you?'
'Fine, thank you.'
'And who is this?'
'My wife.'
'Lovely to meet you…'
'Emily.'
'Emily. I am so, so sorry for the manner of my departure back in
England.'
'No matter. We'll have plenty of time to catch up later. Come, I want
you to listen to my address.'
Utopians assemble excitedly before William.

'Welcome, to Utopia. May your stay here be a happy, and joyous
one. Henry and I, and Emily, and the other islanders would like to
say, how grateful we are, for your company. We have been here for
several months now, and, as you can see, we have tried to make the
place as homely as possible. More huts will be built today,
tomorrow, and through next week, and we will keep clearing the
jungle to continue constructing, orchards, around this dwelling. We
live an easy life, swimming in the morning, resting in the afternoon,
talking at fireside in the evening. Our priest, Manou, always tells us
a story then. We eat fish and fruit, drinking from the nearby stream.
We use the latrines behind me a fair way down that path, and over
there in that direction is a track that leads into the jungle. Money
does not exist here. We have no need for it. Nor religion. Just a
belief in right, goodness, peace, fellowship and love. That is all we
ask for you to observe, nothing more. Once again, welcome.'

Utopians disperse disinterestedly.
Tom eagerly with envelope.

'Heather writes to you.'

"My dear William, it seems an age since you and Henry, with Emily, took that brave step to leave England for a brighter future in the tropics. I have listened daily for any new reports concerning your venture, but I suppose your community is still developing and as such is not demanding the attention it will when you have established a fully-fledged society that we in the outside world might use as benchmark to improve upon matters to which we have grown accustomed."

William looks up at the backs of departing Utopians.

"Tom, as you are aware now you read this, made his return some months ago, but ever does ill fortune seem to dog our brother whither he travels. He had been staying with me not a fortnight when I returned late one evening to find the house ransacked and Tom lying in a heap on the living room floor. When I managed to rouse him, he said he remembered nothing, and with police search finding no signs of forced entry, nothing stolen and in their conclusion motiveless attack, I was left with the burden of many unanswered questions exacerbated only further on discovery that in fact one thing had been taken from the attic room, a portable television set."

William glances at Tom's bag.

"I only noticed because Tom himself in his sojourn with me grew self-confined to the top of the house there. Goodness knows I don't remember him obsessed with television when we were all family at home, but here during his stay with me he would, if he could, watch it all day and all night without cease. Any protestation from me for him to break off viewing would be met with incoherent mutterings such that I feared at times, over this recurrent behaviour, for the very stability of his mood."

William scrutinizes his brother.

"As it fell, Tom's spirit never settled, and it came as little surprise to me when after another fortnight he declared he must leave my home, and indeed England. That his intent was to seek you out in Utopia came as shock to me. Your dreamy nature has ever been at odds with his abject practicality, witness those previous clashes you have endured with him so, and I have seen no evidence to convince me that Tom's attitude has altered at all in this regard."

William studies Tom further.

"As it is, I am glad beyond measure that I have this chance to contact you. Do not trust him, William. Tom's gambling addiction is far from cured. I haven't the time, nor stomach, to give detail but craving still infects his heart making him unpredictable, devious, and rife with recrimination. If he is warm towards you, know he holds cold dagger behind his back, to plunge into yours. Dramatic these words may seem but they reflect only the depth of my concern for the wellbeing of you and your venture. Our brother's influence has always overshadowed your achievements, I would never want his involvement with the seedier side of reality to impinge on your dreams. I still pray though that he may reform enough to settle quietly and peacefully with you, Henry and Emily. All my love, Heather.'

'Is everything alright?'
'Fine. Heather is well.'
'Of what does she speak?'
'Not much.'
'The letter is long, William.'
'And in affection entirely characteristic of our sister.'
'Very well. What are these stories about then?'

Evening comes.
Manou, flames from the fire casting him half in light, half in darkness, tells tale.
Night falls.

Day breaks.
Passes.
Evening comes.
Manou, half in light, half in darkness, tells tale.

Night falls.

Day breaks.
Passes.
Evening comes.
Manou tells tale.
Night falls.

7

Henry and Tom swim.
They emerge from the sea.
'What do you carry in your bag?'
'Why do you ask?'
'You are not without it. Your winnings, perchance?'
'Of sort.'
'You may have fooled William, you know, but I continue to see
straight through you.'
'And miss your own foolishness thereby.'
'What do you mean?'
'She is not in love with you.'
'You don't know what you're talking about.'
'Keep watch, Henry, or I might just spirit her away.'
'She hasn't looked twice at you.'
'No, once was enough.'
Tom heads off to jungle.
Henry enraged, but impotent.
From beach.
Jittery.

Evening comes.
Utopians, except William in his hut, relaxing by the fire.
Manou stands.
Tom emerges from the jungle.
Small sticks in his hands.
'These will make our lives here that much more interesting.'
Henry stands alongside the priest.
'Turn on your heel. We are happy without your prostitution to
chance. No one loses here.'
'Just your shortfall. These people don't want boredom of certainty
but adventure. Risk and reward, my friend.'
'You are none that of mine. Reward we own, by being here. Why do
you come?'
'You share too readily. There are always winners and losers in life.
We play, and those with most straws at end of the day order those

with less to do their bidding in the morning.'
'That is not our way. Now leave!'
William emerges from hut.
'What is it? What's wrong?'
'He wants to gamble.'
'It is the best way.'
'We do not bet, nor do we roll any dice for superiority. Tell him, William.'
'There will be no straws, no chance, and no inequality in our society.'
'Ditch his stories then too.'
'What?'
'He lords it over us, speaks to us like children. The Deep. God. Nothing but scaremongering designed to control. Even you grow bored and hide in your hut.'
'Manou is our priest. He emboldens us. And because of your disrespect I say we will have stories double the time at night. We will lead our simple life during the day too, fishing, eating, swimming and sleeping.'
'No! We do not want that.'
'Well what do you want?'
'Television.'
'Emily.'
'Yes, that is something we need. It is certain too, a great leveler.'
'Indeed, it razes intellect. We have lived here for months without it, and we are fine.'
'For you are content with a life of tedium. I say it would be good for our community. Who agrees?'
'There will be no television on this island. If you want it, return home.'
Tom stalks off into the jungle.
William walks to beach

Benign weather produces beautiful sunset.
Clouds form as night falls.

8

A storm.
Tempest whose intensity rends the sky asunder.
Lightning forks.
Stabs down across the landscape.
William watches from his hut, blinded by torrential rain.
Drenched.
Wind howling.
Seeming sound of wailing.
Utter darkness.
Stars and moons quite blocked out by the thunderclouds.
Lightning sheet, revealing a figure in midst of camp.
Darkness.
Lightning again.
Figure disappearing into jungle.
William rushes after him.
Trips over tree roots.
Flat to his face.
Regains his footing.
Stumbles blindly round in big circle back to camp.
Lightning flash displays the dwelling in its entirety.
Huge television screen positioned in one corner.
Darkness.
Next flash shows the appliance is not there.
Storm begins to blow itself out.
Thunder cracks to lowly rumble.
Lightning loses intensity
Rain lessens.
Wind abates.

9

Day breaks.
William heads to the beach.
Schools of jellyfish are in the shallows.
Shark fins move behind them, a little further out.
William settles, exhausted.
Sleeps.
Dreams.

A man, without face, approaches camp.
Henry's hut.
Draws Emily out.
Leads her into the forest.
William wakes.

Rushes to Henry's hut.
'William. What is it? Emily.'
'She is gone. Taken, my friend.'
A terrifying scream sounds.
Then again.
Henry races into the jungle.
William follows.

They return disconsolate.
Tom is in the dwelling, rising to greet them.
Pinned to the ground quickly by Henry.
'Where is she?'
'Who?'
'My wife. What have you done to her, Ottoway?'
'Nothing. William, I don't know what he's talking about.'
Henry lifts him bodily, thrusts him back to the ground.
'Where is she?!'
'I don't know. I haven't seen her.'
Henry hits him.

'Give me her location, or I will kill you.'

'Henry, that's enough.'

'You've seen the manner in which he appraises her. It is his doing.'

'Tom, did you hear the screams?'

'Yes. God, was that her?'

'Stop the pretence, Ottoway! Stop it now! Where is she?'

'I do not know, Henry. I did not steal her.'

'Then who did? Nobody here is culpable. You yourself told me on the beach you would snatch her away. Now show us where you hide whenever you skulk off from here.'

'No. That is my place. Nobody goes there, but me.'

'You deal with him, William. He is your brother.'

'Where are you going?'

'For a swim.'

'The sea is replete with jellyfish, brought in by the storm.'

'For a wander, then.'

'But of Emily?'

'The same too, I should think.'

'But she cried, for help.'

'And does not, now. Why don't I check the Netherworld, maybe she's down there?'

'Henry.'

'Well really, this is all becoming phrase and fable. He hasn't taken her.'

'Thank you, Henry. Now, I shall show you. Where I go.'

Tom leads Henry away into the jungle.

William, stupefied, remains.

10

Long evening ensues.
No story by the campfire.
Embers reveal a figure, at side of clearing.
'Tom? Is that you? Tom, are you alright?'
Henry moves into the light.
'My friend. How good it is to see you back.'
Henry looks haggard.
Haunted.
Sits in shadows of fire.
William moves towards him.
Halted by gasp from Utopians.
Behind, again, another figure.
Holding portable television set.
Upon it programme vulgar, offensive, idiotic.
Utopians are enraptured.
For long minutes, they watch dumbly.
Without warning, Tom turns the set off.
'It will stop working if not afforded due care and attention.'
Turns to leave.
'Won't you stay?'
'Henry.'
'When will he return?'
'What is wrong with you?'
'Who is he, Ottoway?'
'You know very well. Now stop acting. Let us listen to Manou.'
'We must see, not hear.'
'You may do both, with your imagination.'
'The work is too hard.'
'It is inherent faculty of the mind. No energy is expended to access
it.'
'Please, turn it back on.'
'He has gone.'
'His spirit remains.'
'Pull yourself together, Henry. You're not in control.'
'Nor are you.'

'Henry.'

'Stop saying my name.'

'What the…what has he done to you?'

'The appliance is in charge now.'

'No, it isn't.'

'Its intelligence is sublime.'

'Moronic, Henry. It drip feeds image, sustenance alone for the indolent.'

'It must be our fodder.'

'You take pasture where you like, but I'm not leaving my people.'

'Then perish, like his stories.'

Leaves.

William, once more perplexed, stares after.

Walks to Manou's hut.

The priest kneeling.

'Why do you pray to God, Manou? Why even do you believe in Him?'

'Why do you ask, William?'

'I have lost my brother. Now Henry disappears after him.'

'Yet you remain.'

'I don't understand.'

'Men put faith in men. My treasure is with God. So is yours, I think.'

'What on earth makes you say that?'

'I have been listening.'

'But our friendship is ruined. Emily is gone. Tom has her. Now he owns Henry. How do you remain steadfast, Manou, how maintain faith in the teeth of life's obverse gale?'

'I stay obedient. To His will.'

'Even if it runs roughshod over yours?'

'Especially so, for it is then that I know He works His purpose most acutely.'

'By making you suffer. No, that will not explain my predicament.'

'What will then, William?'

'Science. Its omniscience lays bare your theology.'

'Though it has yet even to fly the nest. Its chirrup for constant satiety lays bare its frailty, and I fear, future enfeeblement. Its paradigms will pass. God remains.'

'But of the misery in existence. There is so much. Its author must be vile.'

'I agree.'

'That God is malign?'

'Not He.'

'I do not understand.'

'His teaching persists, for it is the only reality, though liars and their lies live on in this dreamscape we continue to build without reflection.'

'Why do they watch it so readily?'

'They have put faith in your brother, for he brandishes mesmeric idol in front of them.'

'Will you talk to the people?'

'If they listen not to their ruler, why then to his priest? I will try, for you William.'

11

Utopians assembled.
Manou stands.

'We forget easily. Now, it is time to remember. William and Henry invited us all to Utopia to live together, in peace, in harmony. That sentiment has been lost. Let us recover it, by joining as one to search once more for Emily.'

Tom steps into the clearing with television, screen currently blank. 'The woman is dead. Ottoway's friend strangled her with a snake. I saw him do it, choking her until her face turned blue and her tongue lolled lazy. I am glad I have returned though, and satisfied that my appliance has proven so popular with you all. Abandon the futile search for a corpse, occupy yourselves more fitfully with this life-giving spirit.'
Television turned on.
Sordid horror, crime and negligence of normality runs upon it.
Transmission is suddenly halted.
Utopians wail in grief.
Tom flees.
Utopians gaze at the blank screen.

Henry emerges into the clearing.
'What is happening? Why is everyone so unhappy?'
'The television. It has stopped working. But who cares now that you have returned? Where have you been?'
'The dreams lied to us. Tom didn't abduct Emily. He is innocent. Emily left of her own volition.'
'But you have slain her, Henry.'
'She has left the island, of that I am sure. I plan to search the archipelago.'
'My friend, she has been taken, and murdered, by you.'
Henry grabs William's throat.
'Speak of her death again, Ottoway, and I shall slaughter you.'
Tom reappears.

Manou intervenes.

'You are best friends. And if not, you are still to set example to the camp.'

'She is not on the island. I know it. And I will find her. Tom.'

Henry leaves.

Tom follows, reluctantly.

William leaves habitation.

He wanders in the forest until he is quite lost, emerging at cliff edge.

Waterfalls pour into the below.

William climbs down.

Moves behind the spray.

Cold, clammy rocks alone meet his touch.

He returns to camp.

Television screens everywhere.

Over a hundred at least.

One bigger than all the rest.

Tom busy fiddling with the original television set.

Cables run from it, screen to screen, all finishing at this largest in the corner.

'How on earth have you managed it? Tom, why have you done this?'

'You really don't know, do you?'

'I haven't the first idea.'

Henry appears.

'That's right, William. But your paradise is to be ruined because of it.'

Utopians are busy carving wood into spikes.

Boxes of candles.

Holders.

Incense.

High Screen to be adorned so.

'Stop it. Please.'

'It is your fault.'

'You promulgate this.'

'But it is your mind which birthed it first.'

'What do you mean?'

'Your imagination, William, created this fantasy, and your dreamland now harvests spirit redolent with its fancy. Behold, the screen is their only truth.'

Tom cuts power to the televisions.

The Utopians wail.

He restores it to shambolic programme.

The Utopians cheer.

'Haven't you anything more joyous to broadcast?'

Stony silence gives way to howls of derision.

'They want more tales of hate and betrayal, not less.'

'But of honesty and justice, humility and faith.'

'Anathema, William. Pain, heartache, misery. This is today's Trinity, worshipped by the masses.'

'I don't believe people think so.'

'Let us see, then.'

Cuts power.

Utopians groan.

'Your leader calls for cessation of entertainment. What say you to that?'

Assembled glare with vitriol at William.

Advance towards him.

William flees.

Tom follows, with Henry.

12

They arrive at beach.
Deserted.
Tom is struck by object.
Sharp rock, brandished by William.
Tom falls to ground.
Henry looks strangely at him.
'You have murdered him. Why?'
'He took Emily. He has taken you. And our dream, from us.'
'You have killed him. Why?'
'I just said.'
William looks at his chest, covered in blood.
'I am glad I have slaughtered him. And I will do you too, unless you get out of my sight. Now go!'
Henry retreats, still perplexed.

William returns gingerly to camp.
Televisions screens are off.
Utopians wander lazily up and down, occasionally glancing at the blank screens.
'Would you like to attend his funeral?'
'But he is still on the beach. Henry?'
'Would you like to attend?'
'No.'
'Why not?'
'Because I killed him. Just now. You watched me do it.'
'I thought that was a dream.'
'What?'
'He lives still.'
'What are you talking about? I slew the bastard! Didn't I?'

William rushes back to beach.
Tom's body is gone.
William tries to sleep in hut.
Television screens run loud programmes.
Incessant output of explicit, cruel, abusive material.

Utopians hurl clods of earth upon William's dwelling.
Somehow, he dozes.

Sleeps.
Dreams.
Tom stands over his bed, his head caved in, staring at him.
Wanders round with blood-spattered clothes.
Sways from side to side until he falls and smashes open the rest of
his skull.

William jerks awake.
Rushes outside.
Sees coffin.
Tom lying in state.
Hair tidied.
Mouth closed.
Head covered.
William puts the lid down.
Henry standing right behind it. 'What are you doing, Ottoway?'
'Checking he is dead.'
Henry advances.
William stands his ground.
Henry turns and walks away.
William makes for his hut.
'You're next.'
William spins round.
Henry has disappeared.
William stares at the coffin.
Makes for his hut.

Unable to sleep.
Night falls.

William watches, from his domicile, the ceremony begin.
Utopian pallbearers walk the coffin past each television.
Place it in front of High Screen.
Fall to their knees.
Rise.
Carry the coffin to shallow grave.

Place it in the hollow.

Bury it with earth.

Turn to pelt William's hut with remaining clods.

Henry leads the way. 'Banish him.'

'I would like to hold one last meal, in memory of my brother. To celebrate High Screen's magnificence.'

'He will like that.'

Night falls.

13

Next morning, William walks past High Screen.
Doffs his imaginary hat in mockery.
Stands stock still.
Utopians are right there, in postures of worship, gently lowing.
William sees Manou. 'What are they doing?'
'They seek its blessing, William, for the meal of commemoration tonight.'
'And how will this inanimate make reply?'
'You will be labelled blasphemer if you do not abide, and join their service.'
Utopians sweep in waves now.
Mumbling.
Chanting.
'Raise our Lord.'
Set to building tables and chairs.
William trudges to beach.

Plunges into surf.
Returns to shore to find Manou waiting for him.
'I thought you didn't rise this early.'
'Hello, William.'
'Are you alright?'
'It is a copy. The screen, it mimics. And in imitating, so it distorts.'
'One could say the same of your storytelling.'
'Then your judgement would be, distorted.'
'What difference?'
'Word, and image. When I talk of Netherworld, of the Deep, your imagination is free to devise its own pictures. The screen, however, holds that faculty in thrall. Imagination becomes its slave, consequentially abused by it.'
'But I have been there. It is empty. Cold rock and ice. Like the rest of this cosmos.'
'Wake up!'
William blinded by the sun.
Shades his eyes.

Tom, head smashed in, looms over him.
'Wake up!'
Picks up handful of sand.
'Remember, I will be with you tonight.'
Throws sand in William's face.
William clears it from his eyes.
Beach deserted.
Heads back to camp.

Sees his priest.
'Manou, where did you go?'
'Go?'
'Yes. Why did you leave?'
'But I have been here all the time.'

14

Night falls.
Utopians gather at table.
William strains to see.
Each wears mask of Tom's face.
'Let us begin.'
William sweeps his water melon away.
'Remove your masks. Take them off! Now!'
Henry removes his first.
The others follow.
The same face is painted on their own.
'How did you do it? When did you have time?'
'Tom was most helpful in this regard.'
'What!?'
'He joins us now.'
Tom emerges from his grave.
Utopians cross themselves vigorously.
Tom swings dead body of Emily so it smashes into Manou's head.
Flings her corpse on the table.
Riddled with snake bites.
Henry twists William's arm up beneath his shoulder.
'See what you did, Ottoway.'
'It was him. He.'
Tom has disappeared.
Utopians approach William.
High Screen comes to life.

Gentlemen of profound erudition at conversation round table.
'You've wasted your life.'
Laughter echoes.
William flees.
'You've wasted your life.'
Laughter sounds round him in the forest.
He charges.
Trips.
Falls.

Tom brandishes bamboo cane.

Whips him all down his back.

'You've wasted your life.'

'How? You're not corporeal.'

Tom holds high the original portable set.

'You see, the power of television. It is the only god!'

Tom rushes away into the forest.

William chases.

They approach cliff face.

Tom looks round.

Collides with Henry running from the opposite direction.

Both fall from the top, hitting hard ground in between the waterfalls.

William descends.

The bodies lie at impossible angles, clumsily embracing one another.

Tom rises. 'Do not touch me, for I have not yet returned to the Proselyte.'

William swipes at him.

Tom floats up and away.

William collapses with fatigue.

Sends his dream to the world.

Passes out.

Wakes up on the beach.

Tom sits astride the dead bodies of Henry and Emily.

Burns Manou's Bible the while.

William dives for him.

Tom floats away again, into the surf, the sea.

William follows him.

Picked up by the vessel in which Andrew voyages.

15

Andrew tends William.
William gives up the ghost.
Andrew walks above decks.
Sees huddle round the Captain.
He holds portable device.
The crew are gambling on-screen.
Andrew grabs the appliance.
Throws it over the side.
The sailors hoist him up and over likewise.

Andrew is washed up on Utopia's beach.
Makes his way to the clearing.
Utopians are all lying dead.
High Screen displays still picture of our home.
The Earth.
Its beauty.
Purity.
A hand, blood-soaked, reaches up to its power button.
Drags itself down the screen, drenching it red.
Falls limp.
Andrew moves forward, closing the dead priest's eyes.
Turns the screen off.
Weeps.

RICK WITH A (BIPOLAR) VIEW

1

A large stadium.
A football match.
Rick, a seemingly everyday twenty-something sits high in the stands.
He is trying to keep his attention on the game, but he keeps glancing round nervously.
I tell you, it was so high up you could see the clouds rolling in from all points.
There were thousands and thousands of people,
All with their own problems,
Families,
Past to deal with…
Stop thinking, Rick.
…how does the world keep going?
You know it's no good for you.
How come it's still so ordered when everyone's got so much to deal with?
Electronic music, soft at first, is heard.
How come it's my fault when everything falls apart?

2

A nightclub.
The DJ is halfway through his set.
Clubbers share the same space on the floor.
But they dance individually, increasingly in their own dazed world.
I love house music.
Especially the hard stuff.
You can totally lose yourself in it.
It's like the club becomes your own place.
And then it opens up to become everyone else's place as well.
All as one.
That's the music's magic.
That's what I love most about it.
The oneness.
Absorbing the energy from the dance floor.
Like one happy family.

3

A counselling room.

It is cold.

Bare.

Uninviting.

'What have we been working on for the last few months, Rick?'

Cognition.

'What image, specifically?'

'Turning my downward spiral of negative self-talk into a climbing stairway of positive thought.'

'That's it. That's cognitive therapy. Now what do you do if you feel your panic rising?'

'Admit the feeling.

Don't fight it.

Go with its flow.

Ride that tide.

I am not going mad.'

'Good. You're on the mend Rick, I know it.'

Electronic music, soft at first, is heard.

'Thanks, Dave.'

4

A party.
The DJ plays funky house.
Rick watches him.
'What do you think?'
'I love it.'
'You a clubber?'
He studies him.
'You want to be a DJ.'
'That's more my bag.'
'I can get you a gig if you want. My brother owns a club. Here, have
a go, let's hear you play.'
Rick glances round nervously.
'Now?'
He takes the headphones.
Skims through the vinyl.
Picks a track.
Tees it up, and makes the mix transition smoothly.
He repeats procedure with several more tunes.
'Right, I've seen enough. You're rubbish!'
Rick despairs.
'Only joking, you've got yourself a DJ date this Friday.'

5

Rick's bedroom.
Rick lies on his bed, unable to keep still.
My mind's racing nineteen to the dozen, thinking about the gig.
It's going to be awesome.
Everyone's going to love you.
I can't believe how happy I am all of a sudden.
The whole world will be with you.
My thoughts are racing now.
Charging me round the room.
Bucking me madly.
Until they unseat me to the ground.
Laughing at you.
Rick blacks out.

6

It hits me the second I wake up.

A sweeping motion.

Like the gathering darkness that rushes up on the planet when the moon fully eclipses the sun.

Except there's no light on the other side.

Just continued night.

Heavy blackness.

And a bleakness so terrible it drains all hope and happiness from your lifeblood.

Rick tries to get out of bed.

If I can make it to the door, I'll be alright.

Just lie back, stay there and hide from the world for the day.

No, you're better than that now.

Come on.

Stand up.

One, two, three.

Rick stands.

Just get to the door, and everything will be fine.

No, no, you'll only open it and feel terrible.

Be quiet.

The doorbell sounds.

Rick is terrified.

'Rick, Jimmy's here.'

'I'll just grab some clothes.'

Rick turns to his wardrobe.

Opens its doors.

The decision hits me right in the face.

Come on, Rick, it's only clothes.

It doesn't matter what you choose.

But it does, it does.

If you wear the blue shirt and your jeans then you might be unhappy for the rest of your life.

Don't be silly.

You're stronger than this.

Rick puts his hand on the blue shirt.

Then takes the white one and his jeans.
I need to see Dave.

7

A common room.
It is warm.
Cosy.
Friendly.
We're listening to Anne.
She's in a pretty bad way.
The illness has got her good and proper at the moment.
Clawing away.
Refusing to let go.
She's much further down the line than I am today.
I mean, she's suicidal.
She's really going to do it.
You can tell from what she's saying that the depression has killed
her hope.
And this is the same woman who was feeling all right last week.
Speaking words of encouragement to those of us who were suffering
as she does now.
We listen to her.
Nod in agreement.
Sympathy.
Empathy.
Anything but offering suggested solutions to her problems.
She needs to immerse herself in the depression.
Let it wash over her.
Then find her own way out.
And this facility provides space for such expression.
A safe environment for patients to develop a relationship with their
illness, aided by the help and support of its staff and attendant
psychiatrists.
You see, we patients, we believe the world's a threat, an
environment which can only damage us.
It makes us fearful.
Paranoid.
Robbing us of our right to exist.
That's why places like this are so important for us, to take some of

the self-imposed weight off our shoulders.
It's home.
I feel happy there.
It's always a wrench to leave.

8

Friday.
The nightclub.
Its resident DJ is building to the end of her set.
This is the moment I've been waiting for.
She beckons Rick to the turntables.
He glances round nervously, heading over.
Stands in the booth.
Blinks out at the crowd.
And that's it.
I'm in control.
I start slowly, but the occasion soon overtakes me, and before long
I'm letting rip with some belters, playing one thumper after the
other.
Long, low, deep rumbling breaks.
Building higher and higher.
I'm teasing the crowd.
Lifting them up.
Bringing them out of themselves and along with me on my sonic
odyssey into trance.
The atmosphere's electric.
It must be a hundred and ten degrees, with the sweat dripping off the
walls and people pouring water all over themselves to cool down.
Three o'clock.
Three in the morning, when all the drunks have left the pub, had
their kebabs and fights and passed out on their sofas, and all the
commuters are safely tucked up in bed with their partners, after
dinner, a bottle of wine and a film about this crazy world we live in.
We're going mad.
Mental.
Taking ourselves away from what's outside.
To a place where everyone loves each other.
And the beat is ruler of all.
I bring my set to a crescendo, finishing with a manic crash.
The crowd gawp.
Clap.

Cheer me to the rooftops.

9

Rick's bedroom.
Rick lies on his bed.
He is unable to sleep.
Never give up fighting…
Ride the tide.
But remember…
It was awesome.
Everyone loved you.
Sometimes the only way to win…
The whole world is with you.
Is to lie down…
Laughing at you.
And surrender.
Thanks for the white flag.
Electronic music, soft at first, is heard.

BREAK OUT THE BUBBLY!!

1

A dead-end town.
Two competing shops stand opposite one another.
Adrian's is in pristine condition.
Sheila's dilapidated.
In here, Emily Tranter serves on its front till.
She is processing Cynthia's groceries.
The tannoy system blares.
Emily Tranter! Emily Tranter! Report immediately to the Manager's Office.
'Is that you, dear?'
'She's got it wrong, as usual. She thinks I'm on the shop floor.'
Emily! To the Manager's office. Now!
'You'd better go along. We'll be alright here for a moment, won't we?'
Almost all the other customers murmur their approval.
Except one.
'No, we most certainly will not. The girl is here to work. She must do her job or find some other assistant to do it for her.'
Cynthia bridles.
'Who are you?'
'Judith Osgood, of course. Now get out of my way, you silly little woman.'
'Your lack of compassion is demonstrable.'
'And your tolerance effeminate.'
'I beg your pardon.'
'Look…'
'Cynthia.'
'Exactly.'
'What?'
'That says it all.'
Emily spies her colleague approaching.

'Ginger, thank you. Tabatha's just called me to the…'
But Ginger has sailed straight past!
Tranter! Office! Now!
Mrs. Osgood is looking round disapprovingly.
'Where is that noise coming from?'
'Go on, Emily, you must obey your summons.'
Emily signs off, lifts the hatch, slips past Mrs. Osgood and heads to the office.
The door sticks as she pushes it open.
Her Assistant Manager turns away suspiciously from a monitor, almost knocking the glass of whiskey she has next to her onto the floor.
'Ah, about time. What were you doing out there?'
'I was on the front till, Tabatha. What is that?'
Tabatha consults a chart full of messy scribblings.
'I thought Ginger was on duty there this morning. Anyway, you're here now.'
'It's complete chaos in the shop, and she hasn't offered to help at all.'
'Of course she hasn't. Honestly Emily, sometimes I really do wonder at your ability to judge other people.'
Emily's jaw drops open.
'Now, there's a new employee starting today.'
Emily's jaw falls even wider agape.
'You know, member of staff.'
'I know what you mean Tabatha, I just didn't know we were recruiting at the moment.'
'Well I'm sorry we didn't consult you on the matter. Carol should have run it past you first, of course.'
'Maybe she should have, or we might get another Sarah. Are you spying on us?'
'Are you still here?'
'You haven't told me where to meet this new, employee.'
'Staff room. And be welcoming. This one's important.'
Emily frowns.

2

She heads to the staff room.

Matthew, a handsome young man, knocks her off guard with his smile.

'Are you all right?'

'I'm fine. Can I help you?'

'I hope so. It's my first day.'

'But you're a boy.'

'Last time I looked.'

'I mean, Carol doesn't employ men.'

'Well, she hired me. Look, she even gave me this uniform.'

'How the…you'd better follow me.'

'I'm Matthew.'

'Emily. Emily Tranter.'

She leads him from the staff room, wondering why her name suddenly sounds so strange in the utterance.

'There are five aisles. Milk and dairy in the first. Fruit and vegetables second. Bread and condiments down there. Meat and frozen, fourth. And drinks and household plus the lottery kiosk last. Sarah, this is Matthew. He's our new colleague.'

Sarah is looking straight down at the floor.

'Nice to meet you.'

'Come on.'

They move from earshot.

'She used to be really happy, quiet but positive. Then she started turning up late, even miss whole shifts, never with word of apology.'

'Have you asked her why?'

'She won't tell us, and no one's got the time to spend with her. The shop's not performing well and we're stretched to the limit. Well, that's the tour. I'll ask Tabatha where she'd like you to start working.'

The Manager, Carol, storms towards them.

'Emily! We're having a meeting. Hello, Matthew.'

'Hi, Carol.'

'Well what are you gawping at, Tranter? Go and get the room set up.'

'But it's the middle of the day. The shop's wide open.'
'I've closed it. Come on now, get to it. I need to speak to Matthew. Go on, then.'
Emily pauses, then makes her way to the boardroom.

3

The boardroom is already set up fine.

Matthew and Sarah enter, then Ginger, Tabatha and last of all Carol.

Emily looks round.

'Where are the other staff?'

'I've sent them home.'

'But we're mid-shift.'

Ginger is filing her nails.

'Why are we here, Carol?'

'Sit down. All of you. Come on. Right, this is important.'

Carol breathes deeply.

'I've come in on my day off to tell you, so listen up.'

Suddenly, she bursts into tears.

Heaving groans.

Gut-wrenching sobs that force her to the floor where she rolls round uncontrollably.

Tabatha, first to react, seeks to console her.

'F**k off!'

'Carol, that's enough.'

'Is it you? Are you the thief?'

'Now you know I'm not. We've been through this already.'

'Then which one of them is the culprit?'

Ginger is twining her hair.

'Has someone been nicking the champagne again?'

'Yes, Ginger, they have and do you know why that matters? Because this is my shop. Which means one of you is stealing from me. Again.'

'No we aren't.'

'Do you know how retail operates?'

Tabatha sighs.

'Who are you talking to, Carol?'

'There are constituent parts to the business. Revenue, for example. Profit. Profit margin. Assets. Equity. Market value. Earnings per share. Return to investors. Are you with me?'

Ginger is again busy with her nails.

'We don't have any investors. What you see is what we've got.'

'So if the champagne continues to disappear I will be forced to downsize, us.'

'Well the temps can go first.'

'That won't be enough.'

Ginger preens.

'I'm not going anywhere. I've been here longest, after Tabatha.'

'Great,' sighs Emily, 'so Sarah and I get the boot.'

'And him.'

'He stays. Who's stealing the champagne? Who the f**k is it?'

'Nobody knows, Carol. We didn't find out last time, and chances are we won't now.'

Ginger is twirling her hair.

'Is that why you're watching our everyday? Great entertainment that must be, I mean who needs a load of morons talking crap round some jacuzzi when you can have it all here, at *Sheila's*, without paying the licence fee?'

'It's not on the BBC actually,' Emily sniffs, 'and Big Brother is an Orwellian concept, not the brainchild of some illiterate executive.'

'You're going to fail that adult ed. course Tranter, just like everything else you've ever attempted in your life. I was talking about *Love Island* anyway.'

Carol lashes out at Tabatha.

'It's you! You're swiping it.'

'No, I am not.'

'You're guilty as sin, you thieving cow! You're tending me to throw everyone off the scent.'

Tabatha stands up firmly.

'I'm not taking any more of this nonsense. We both know who's behind this, but instead of doing the honourable thing you're dragging these poor girls into your mess.'

'Get out! Get the hell out of my shop!'

Carol launches herself at Tabatha.

Matthew tackles Carol into the side table, motioning at Sarah to Emily.

'Look after her. Don't let her out of your sight.'

Emily gawps at Sarah.

Ginger is strangely stricken.

Carol struggles beneath Matthew, still shouting at her Assistant Manager.

'You're fired! Employment terminated. Get out of my employ!'

'I've already resigned. Twenty years of service and this is how you repay me. You need help. You're not fit for purpose.'

Tabatha walks.

Carol sobs hysterically.

Matthew comforts her.

Emily is dazed.

'It's alright. She's been like this before. Where's Sarah?'

'She was here. She was just here.'

'Find her. You must stop her.'

'Why? What the hell's going on, Matthew?'

'Just find her. And take her to the staff room. I'll meet you there.'

Emily races away, searching high and low, ending up at the front till where she spies Sarah opposite, perched on a ground floor window ledge of *Adrian's*.

Emily rushes over, straight past Cynthia outside, she stunned by proceedings.

4

Marvilyn is on front till, reading a novel.
'Oh, it's you again. Check all you want, we don't care anymore.'
'I'm not here for price comparison! I need to see Adrian.'
'Why?'
'Just take me to him. Please.'
Marvilyn studies Emily over her pince-nez, then leads her from the
till upstairs.
'Marvilyn.'
Up another flight of stairs.
'Marvilyn!'
Emily reaches the attic.
It is dark and dank.
Haunting.
Large, stacked wooden crates occupy the area.
Emily bumps into one, hearing the sound of bottles chinking inside.
She comes to her senses.
'Ground level, she's on the ground level.'
She races back downstairs, bursting into the first room she reaches.
Sarah is out on its window ledge.
'Thank goodness. You're alright.'
'Nice of you to say so, but I really won't be fine until this woman
leaves my office.'
'That woman, Adrian, is Sarah Strumsum, and she's my colleague.
Sarah, please come in from there.'
'Yes, do. Then we can all have a cup of tea, to calm yourselves
down. Marvilyn.'
Marvilyn enters.
Curtsies.
'My lord.'
'Tea for two. Or three. Why are you out there? What's your
problem?'
'They hate me. Every last one of them. They're pinning the blame on
me. I won't have it anymore.'
'I see. Look, there are two ways you can leave my premises, down
there or through here. Make your mind up, and get on with it.'

Adrian returns to his papers.

Emily moves towards Sarah who nears further the edge.

'I know who it is. I've got proof. It's a horrible thing. Why did they have to blame me?'

'No one's blaming you. Let's go back to *Sheila's* and sort it out.'

'I'm not going there again. It's a coven of witches. Those bullies, I despise them.'

Sarah jumps, falling into soft bushes.

Emily races from the room.

Adrian glances up.

'Close the window, would you Marvilyn? Get the tea, then come and see me about these disappointing sales figures of yours.'

'As you wish, my lord.'

5

Emily arrives at the bushes, but Sarah has disappeared.
Tabatha approaches.
'Sarah,' cries Emily, 'have you seen Sarah?'
'She's at the kiosk. Just returned. Why?'
'She's back at work!?'
'Yes. What's the matter?'
'I don't…is Carol all right?'
'Yes, she's fine now. She's just worried about the thefts.'
'Why was she accusing you, Tabatha?'
'I'm her Deputy. She leans on me.'
'But she's breaking your back.'
'Do you remember before, when this happened, what was going
wrong for her?'
Emily swallows.
'She was separating from David.'
'Yes. But there was a time prior to that also, when we first opened
the store. The champagne went missing straightaway.'
'Is that why CCTV's been installed?'
'You must understand the pressure, Emily. Targets haven't been met
for months. The shop is heading for closure. Then our most
expensive item starts going walkabout.'
'Sarah said she was being bullied. Why, Tabatha?'
'She found out. Caught her in the act.'
'Who?'
'Why, Carol of course.'

6

Emily approaches the office.

Carol wrenches the door open, almost sent flying backwards when it sticks.

'You're late.'

'I was looking for Sarah. She was over at Leafy Hollow's.'

'Don't call him that. He has a name, you know.'

'What's wrong, Carol?'

'I can't work in this sty. Why is Tabatha so completely disorganised? I shall have to have words with her tomorrow.'

'You've just fired her.'

'Well after that, then.'

Emily rolls her eyes.

'Why am I here?'

Carol fishes out a piece of paper.

'Here. You'd better get started.'

'By Friday?'

'Well it won't be much good if we have it on Saturday now, will it?'

'But I hate parties, Carol, you know that.'

'All the more reason to get stuck in organising one. Everyone celebrates New Year.'

'Why can't Ginger do it?'

'She's not capable.'

'Matthew?'

'He's only just joined.'

Ginger enters, smirking.

'Ah, Tranter, follow me.'

'Since when do you tell me what to do?'

Ginger points to her Assistant Manager badge.

'You promoted her!?'

'Yes, yes. Just get on with it. Go with her.'

'No.'

'Do you value your career?'

'It's a job, Carol.'

'Which pays for your bedsit accommodation. How would you like to lose that?'

'I'd be happy to, actually.'

'You've no family here, Tranter, no lover, no friends. Where would you go? Exactly. So just follow Ginger, and do what she says.'

She grabs Tabatha's bottle of whiskey from the table, returning her attention to the CCTV.

Emily opens her mouth to protest, then trails Ginger from the office.

'Aisle one. It's a mess.'

'So?'

'So clean it up. And see that it's stocked, quick. You've got four more to go after that.'

'The whole shop?'

'Carol's cleared half the staff today. With Tabatha gone and Matthew next to useless, that leaves you, me, Sarah and that weird woman who used to work across the road. The oddball, Tranter, who can't get her nose out of a book.'

'Marvilyn!?'

'Go figure. But that's the kind of thing that happens when the boss is more miserable than the bloody weather's been since god knows when. She's on front till. Go look for yourself.'

'You go look.'

'No, you go look.'

'Stop ordering me around, Ginger.'

Ginger points to her badge.

'Just clean aisle one.'

'No.'

'Yes.'

'No.'

'Yes.'

'No.'

Starr! Tranter! Stop arguing.

They look towards the office where Carol has the microphone at her mouth.

Get in here! The pair of you. Now!

They enter, Emily sullen.

'You could have just come out and told us to knock it off.'

'Shut up! Shut up, Tranter! Shut the f**k up!'

'You're still on the microphone.'

Carol hurls it to the ground.

Adrian picks it up.

'How the…how did he get here?'

'He works here. He's the Assistant Manager.'

'No, I'm the Assistant Manager.'

'Yes, yes, to him.'

Emily laughs.

'So that makes you, what, the Assistant Assistant Manager?'

'I'm still higher in the pecking order than you.'

'Actually, you can be as well.'

'But you promoted me. Over her.'

'Of course. I think it would be good if there were three of you.'

'Who's the other one?'

'Matthew.'

'But he's only been here five minutes. How can he be Assistant Assistant Manager too? What the f**k is going on?'

She storms off.

Emily sighs.

'What is going on, Carol? Ginger's right. How can there be three Assistant Assistant Managers? And how can he be the Assistant Manager when he doesn't even work here? And how come Marvilyn's manning the front till?'

A scream sounds from there sending them all running towards it.

Adrian notices Cynthia moving away.

'Marvilyn, why is that champagne bottle down your blouse?'

'My lord?'

Carol grabs it.

She turns it upside down and smacks the bottom hard.

'What do you see? What do you see?'

'Nothing,' sighs Ginger, 'it's empty.'

'Exactly.'

'Well that clears that one up then.'

'The shop's closed. I'm shutting up for the rest of the day.'

Adrian is aghast.

'But it's ten in the morning.'

'Come on, all of you, out. To the boardroom.'

Carol herds the customers from the premises, including a still retreating Cynthia.

7

The boardroom.
Adrian leans forward.
'Let's get this over with so we can open the shop back up again.'
'No one's opening the shop. Not until someone's fessed up. Who are you?'
'I'm Marvilyn. You just saw me. You hired me this morning.'
'You're fired.'
'You can't fire me. Adrian's in charge.'
'Then go and work back there.'
Ginger stops filing her nails.
'I thought he was our new Assistant Manager. How can he be your boss?'
'We're in partnership.'
'When did this happen?'
'It's been months in the offing. Only someone totally unaware wouldn't have seen it coming.'
Emily gapes.
'Well I didn't know we were getting bought out.'
Carol suddenly bursts into tears, heaving, gasping for breath.
Adrian tries to console her.
'It's all right. It's going to be all right.'
Ginger is curling her hair.
'I don't believe this. History's supposed to stay in the past.'
'What are you talking about?'
'Carol gets herself a boyfriend then goes mad when he sells her out.'
Carol frees herself and goes for Ginger.
Matthew restrains her.
'Get off me, Osgood! Get the f**k off me!'
'Just calm down.'
'Osgood? Was that your mum in here this morning?'
'He's a favour. For her deficiency.'
'What? What does she mean, Matthew?'
'You're at it too, Tranter. Don't play the innocent.'
'I don't know what you're talking about.'
'You're f**ing my husband! How much clearer do you want me to

be?'

Matthew moves back.

'That's right, my boy, you're not her only prince.'

'That's enough, Carol. We need to reopen the shop.'

'Who put you in charge?'

'You did.'

'But we haven't unmasked the culprit. Who's the thief?'

'There's only one person in disguise here, Carol. It's time to remove it, then retrieve the stash from mine.'

'You bastard! How dare you expose me?

She glares uneasily.

'Out! Everyone get out! I need to be alone with my thoughts.'

'Is that a good thing?'

'Get out! All of you. Now!'

8

Emily and Matthew return from lunch.

The shop is in immaculate condition.

'What the hell's going on? The shelves, they're all in order.'

They look at each other, rushing round to aisle five where the drinks shelves are completely empty.

'What on earth has she done with it all?'

They hear the sound of the office door sticking, racing back to see Carol stacking boxes against it, trying to shut them out.

Drink bottles cover all floor space, climbing the wall to ceiling level.

Emily gulps.

'What are you playing at?'

'Preparing the party.'

'In here?'

Carol nods furiously.

'But where will people sit?'

'We don't need tables.'

'How are people going to eat, Carol?'

'We're not having a meal.'

'But it's a party.'

The Manager roars with laughter.

'Eating at parties went out with the Ark, Tranter. These days we dance, and we do that until we drop.'

'But you're forty three.'

Matthew struggles to keep a straight face.

'You can't store the whole drinks aisle in here. I don't understand, Matthew. What's she doing?'

Adrian enters, pushing them in.

'We have to put it back.'

Tabatha, Ginger and Cynthia enter quickly, the latter only just squeezing into the tiny space left.

She giggles.

'It's like a nightmare game of sardines.'

Adrian laughs.

'Let's hope we don't all have to kiss the first one in here. Who was the first?'

Everyone looks at Carol.

Carol glares at Cynthia.

'Who are you?'

'I'm Cynthia.'

'You're fired.'

'I don't work here.'

'Who are you then?'

'A paying customer, completely flummoxed by the madness in this place.'

Carol looks at her quizzically.

'Right, welcome to the last meeting of the calendar year. No agenda I'm afraid, my apologies for its absence.'

She laughs manically

'What's wrong with you all?'

Her face falls.

'Look, this is not easy for me. I have not been in the best frame of mind recently.'

She pauses.

'I'm retiring.'

Emily groans.

'But this is your life.'

'It's making me miserable. I keep losing my temper. And I've been horrid to you. Let me explain.'

'If I may,' interrupts Cynthia, 'I think everyone here has some notion of ongoing occurrence. To listen to you confess your soul will surely do you, more than anyone here, no good at all. As far as I know, you have been stealing from yourself. Ergo, you have been hurting yourself, not others.'

Ginger baulks.

'Speak for yourself, old woman. You're not the one who's been slaving away for years running the freak show whilst the management take it in turns to go potty. It's bad enough having to work in this sh**hole with the boss losing her marbles every five minutes and her slashing it up the wall the other fifty five, but then we have to listen to Miss Bedsit-boring droning on in self-pity and self-loathing, and now we have her stumbling round in the middle of us like some scapegoat to the slaughter.'

'Who are you talking about?'

'Strumsum, the poor cow. She's saddled with all the guilt and sin whilst the lot of you, the tribe, get off scot free. Don't think I don't know about all this God crap. I get how it works. It makes the weak-willed feel better about themselves by thinking they can scab a ride to la-la-land by singing a few Hell Mary's!!'

'You're fired.'

'What? You can't do that.'

'And about time too.'

'Shut up, Tabatha. I don't have to listen to you again, ever, thank God.'

'That's right. Because you're fired. And Tabatha's hired again instead.'

'But you gave her the boot. She gave you the boot.'

'Who's the tribal scapegoat now, Ginger?'

'F**k off, Tranter! And f**k you all. This place won't last five minutes without me. Good luck when you hit the wall.'

She leaves, trying to slam the door, which sticks.

'She's rather unpleasant.'

'Stifling, Adrian.'

She smiles.

'Come on Emily, we've still got a party to prepare.'

'You're going to help me?'

'We all will. Together. As a community.'

'Come off it, Carol. We're not even close. And you're retiring anyway.'

'I've changed my mind. Sorry, Adrian.'

She breaks open a bottle of bubbly, pouring a glass for Cynthia.

'Cynthia, you're hired!'

Adrian bristles.

'Wait a minute…'

'You'll have to go too, Matthew. It's *Sheila's* only from here on in.'

'But I…'

'Come on Adrian, let's leave the ladies to it.'

Puts his arm round him.

'Now, tell me about this name of yours.'

'You know it.'

'The Leafy one.'

Adrian glares at Carol.

Matthew winks at Emily.

'Cheers!'

SAMAN'S REVENGE

1

A mid-sized village.
Among commercial premises along its parade, an antiques shop.
In its front window, a small but precious looking box.
A large banner hangs taut between two other shops.
All Hallows Festival.
Lit by murky morning dawn, from which mist a Trustle skips into view.
The horns on its head twitch.
With small hammer, it bangs hard on the ground.
Another Trustle skips past.
Several more follow.
Then a full battalion of the creatures pours along the parade.
They are fleeing from enemy incursion.
Legions of Shifters, chameleon in their essence.
At once visible to the eye, at the next transparent.
Their cry, a hideous ululation in grim parody of those they pursue.
Their leaders driving great beasts before them.
Foul, salivating, red-eyed gargantuans.
And Baturbal, master in command, sweeping on behind.
He carries the Pagos stone, a glowing blue orb matched only in intensity by the bright compass he wields in his other hand.
Its surface shimmers.
Ripples.
The arm swings wildly.
And then they vanish.

2

The fairground is in full swing.
Norman's glasses fall as he climbs off the merry-go-round.
Jack picks them up.
'Come get 'em, coward.'
Jack heads into the darkness of the green, illuminated only marginally by a bonfire burning close to clump of bushes.
Norman's brother, Mark, pursues.
'Give them back to him.'
'Don't they look nice though?'
'You're too stupid to wear them, Jack.'
The two of them fall to fighting.
'Mark, please. Roxie! Help!'
The bushes rustle violently.
A sharp cry pierces the air as a small, hunched figure pushes the scrub apart, his face covered by the cowl of a great, black cloak.
Jack laughs.
'Who the hell are you?'
'I am Saman.'
The old man lifts fingers to the hood of his cloak, removing it sharply to reveal a face worn beyond age, scarred with deep lines which grind viciously into his death-white skin.
Roxie appears, revulsed by the stranger.
Saman studies them in turn.
'Tell me of Shadyridge.'

Shadyridge is the large hill which overlooks the village, Rathe.
On its flat top surface stand two temples.
The huge Olympeon.
The smaller Bellanon.
Ingot is playing at soldiers with his two brothers, Musfel and
Winbat, who are together ranged against him, driving him back
further and further towards Bellanon.
'Ingot.'
'It won't hurt.'
'Father said…'
'Just a minute.'
Ingot stands in the near darkness of the temple.
A magnificent frieze adorns its south wall, depicting the Earth-
goddess Thera appearing from the ground as Trustles on each side of
her bang their hammers on the floor.
Near to the frieze a fifty foot high golden statue, again of the Earth-
goddess, stands proudly.
Between them both lies a small room, screened from view by a thick,
red curtain.
Ingot approaches.

*As Ingot grew into a fearsome young warrior, so the dark forces
away in the wastes of Zon, roused from slumber by this threat
perceived, knew in their malice only one response.*

Basturbal's army heads for Shadyridge.
The Pagos Stone glowers, shooting blue light from its orb.
The compass arm swings ever more violently between its cardinal
points.
Troops take up defensive positions, Ingot and his two brothers with
their father Volcrix:

Be brave, my sons, in battle. Remember that he who is bold, the gods

*will favour, he who is valiant the gods will reward. Surrender not
your weapon, nor yourself, but fight on until victory is ours.*

The young warrior looks to Olympeon, its gateway to the heavens
opened.
On the upper level, The Circle of Lore, giant figures move in sombre
fashion.
They begin to ascend.
Thrackan remains, spying the Pagos Stone.
Ingot watches the god of war raise his hand to deflect its light into
Bellanon, penetrating the temple's wall.
He sheaths his sword, hurtling over the hilltop.
Inside, the Chief Elder see Thera's frieze lit bright blue, her
depiction animated.
She scowls down upon him.
'Open the box.'
'But your decree.'
'Allow him to see.'
Ingot enters.
Prowls.
'I have been expecting you.'
The Chief Elder swallows.
'The Abormine Oracle told me that you would fulfil your destiny
here today.'
The warrior moves towards the curtain, through it.
Two thick candles stand atop an altar, a small but precious looking
box perched thereon.
Ingot's hand rests on the lid.
He lifts it.
Outside the room, a surge of energy blows the Chief Elder clean off
his feet.
Ingot throws back the curtain and marches straight past, an aura of
unworldliness, even majesty about him.
Atop Shadyridge, the sky has darkened as a tempest rends the
heavens, thunderbolts raining down to strike both armies
indiscriminately.
Ingot watches then gapes upwards, his arms outstretched:

Now fulfil your prophecy, gods! Now bring succour and relief to these your people who are so mercilessly battered before you.

The storm grows to fever pitch, the thunderbolts suddenly striking deep into the hearts of Basturbal's troops alone.
Shadows appear, felling them with weapons of mist and vapour so that they start to flee back across the hill, driven off by Ingot butchering his enemy without mercy.
He comes across his father lying dead on the battlefield.
Dropping down beside him, he takes his hand in his own, wipes the blood from his brow then rises slowly as the rain continues to lash down from the sky.
The clouds above part hurriedly and as Ingot stares into the void great blocks of dazzling light flood down to fill his mortal frame.
For long moments, he is suffused by the rays, then at last the light recedes and the sky clears.

Ingot's wild and fiery expression had been replaced by a look of the most exquisite tranquility.
Basturbal's army was in full regress.
Soundly defeated.

Saman stokes the now dying bonfire.
He studies the youngsters, they transfixed.

When Ingot returned to Rathe, he naturally enjoyed his share of adulation as the bold warrior who had fought so valiantly in the fray. Some of the soldiers, however, had seen the shafts of light fill his body, and the first rumours of a gift from the gods were seemingly verified by the fact that whatever enterprise the young man turned his attention to was always more than impressively finished.

Within days of the end of the battle, he constructed various weapons that were unparalleled across the land for workmanship and durability. He designed defences of which men had never dreamed, and fully secured Rathe's borders against any further intrusion. On the river Sepui in the west, he was responsible for planning and building ships of enormous size, both military and civil.

As the years passed, Ingot settled into the autumn of his life as contented a man as ever there was, before or since. When at last the time came for him to pass from this world unto the next, an air of immortality settled itself around his dying person. "I see the gods waiting to greet me, brothers."

'He passed away accordingly.'
Saman is silent.
'Is that it?'
'There is more.'
'So tell us, old man.'
Thunder sounds in the distance.
Saman stands.
'The storm now is as then.'
'What are you on about?'
'Defy the gods. Open the box. Live blessed as Ingot.'
What do we care about him?
'You are his brothers.'
Rain starts to fall.
He suddenly disappears into the gloom.
'Wait!'
Mark scours the bushes.
'He's gone.'
Storm prevails.
Norman grabs his brother's arm.
'We need to leave, Mark.'
'We'll meet back here, tomorrow morning, eleven o'clock. What's the matter?'
'I thought I...did you see it, Roxie?'
'Come on, we need to get inside.'
They leave, Jack separately.

4

Roxie, Mark and Norman stand by the cold ashes of the bonfire.
Jack approaches.
'So what the hell are we doing back here?'
'Looking for Saman.'
'You what? The guy's long gone, him and his crackpot story. What is it?'
'Go on, Rox.'
'I know the tale. It's in a history book, in the library.'
'So he cribbed it. Sounds about right.'
'Where are you going?'
'There. It's opening time.'
'There's more, though.'
'I'm not interested.'
'To the story. Pages after Ingot's death.'
'So what happened?'
'I don't know. I stopped at the exact point Saman did last night. I was spooked then, and I'm frightened now. We need to go back.'
'Well you can count me out.'
'You don't have to come with us. Tud's Tower. It's a conduit, remember?'
'In your imagination, Carter.'
The sky suddenly darkens.
The wind picks up and rain begins to fall.
'This is ridiculous. Are you sure that storm guy's not still in the bushes? I'm off, anyway. See you later.'
'The Tripsy Inn's that way.'
'Home. I need a rest to get over all this excitement.'
He leaves, Mark watching him suspiciously.
Weather worsens.
'We should get inside.'
'The library. Come on, we can get there before it really starts pouring. What's wrong?'
'I'm going for it, Rox. Come on, Norman.'
'I'd prefer to go to the library.'
'I need you with me. You know how to get to Tud's Tower.'

'But we can't leave Roxie.'

'That's right Mark, you can't leave.'

'He's gone for the prize.'

'And I'm yours.'

'You'll be fine.'

'What is it with you two?'

'I can't let him win.'

'Why not?'

'Look, we'll go to Tud's Tower. I'll check in with you there. If you need me, if Jack's gone on, we'll come back.'

'And if you do cross paths?'

'I'll send Norman back.'

'Great.'

'Well I don't care. It's obviously going to be tipping it down all day today anyway. I'd rather be indoors.'

Roxie heads for the library, Mark in the opposite direction.

Norman hesitates, looking after them both, then follows his brother.

5

Jack stands before the oak door of the tower.
He grabs the handle and pulls it roughly, a fierce gust of wind blowing into him against which he enters to find a small, dimly lit room with large bed in one corner.
Soft breeze blows down a set of stairs that winds into the floor above.
Jack climbs into a darker, bare room, from which further staircase winds upwards.
He climbs once more, struggling into pitch blackness.
Winds blow hard into him.
He notices a soft glimmer of light in the middle of the ceiling.
Moving towards it, he bumps into an object directly underneath the glow and leaning forward he looks into a shallow pool of water clearing before his eyes.
Jack is amongst other deities in the Circle of Lore.
He looks towards Bellanon.
The Chief Elder stands with Ingot.

It is Thrackan, not I who should bear penalty. His is the crime. Let him pay the price.

Jack picks up a large, round stone.
The water shimmers slightly.

I was immortal and omnipotent. Nothing could harm me. Nothing.

Thera bows her head.
Jack lifts his arm and lets the stone fly.

6

Mark and Norman study the bed.
'Who do you think sleeps there?'
'Let's just check the rest of the place out.'
They climb to the first floor, then to the top, moving towards the basin.
They look into its water, seeing Roxie in the library.

Here tell in my words of a battle like no other, when the brave warrior Ingot defeated the Dark Lord Basturbal and enjoyed victory spoils for the rest of his days. I was his protector, the Chief Elder of Rathe, guardian forever of Thera's sacred box. This is my story also.

Roxie turns the pages.

On a cold and blustery day, not long after the battle against Basturbal had been won, Ingot came to Bellanon to seek my advice. "O noble elder, what am I to do now I have gazed in Thera's box, to discover only what the gods know?" "It will become clear to you Ingot, but you must wait." "For how long? Already people speak of a gift from above that sets me apart. Some are happy for me, but my brothers Musfel and Winbat look strangely upon me now."

The water shimmers imperceptibly.

"Trade. We will do business, not make war with our neighbours." "There shall be peace, and your name will be honoured." "There shall be peace, and the people of Rathe will praise the Chief Elder."

The floor begins to tremble.
The tower shakes violently.
Norman and Mark, terrified in the darkness, head for the stairwell.
The oak door slams shut below them.
Weighty clomp of footsteps reverberates through the steps on which they perch.
They retreat, hiding in the pitch black.
A creature, rasping noisily, enters the room.
It sniffs the air with terrific snorts, then heads for the basin.

The brothers bolt down the stairwell, their pursuer right behind them, spluttering, salivating, its eyes glowing red in the darkness.

They stumble towards the door.

Mark lifts the latch.

The oak swings back.

And suddenly they are outside and running up the track.

There is movement ahead of them, then to the side.

Suddenly a Shifter leaps out from the trees pinning Norman to the ground, its very essence changing from dark shadow to transparency to shadow again.

Mark launches himself at the foe, bundling him from his brother.

He sees darkness.

Then forest.

Then darkness again before something kicks it away.

'Come on,' says Jack, helping his rival up, 'let's get out of here.'

7

"There shall be peace, and the people of Rathe will praise the Chief Elder." He bowed his head and a moment of the most profound calm descended upon us, then suddenly I heard a loud crack behind me like the noise of breaking bones. It was the statue of Thera, and it was coming to life! I couldn't believe my eyes. The vast sculpture that stood fifty feet high and weighed so much that every man, woman and child in Rathe had been conscripted to work together to drag it up to Bellanon was being riven from inside, deep stress fractures cutting down through its golden arms until they both suddenly exploded – there, beneath, the limbs were covered with the armour of battle holding an iron spear and shield.

Striving to break free further, the creature within the statue tore to pieces the gold on its legs as it kicked out with flailing armour-clad limbs of enormous size and strength. I tried to shield myself from the falling fragments but I couldn't stop myself from gazing at the amazing transformation that was taking place before my eyes, its torso now shattering to send splinters of gold crashing through the beautiful frieze of our Earth—goddess, itself smashing to smithereens on the cold stone floor of the temple.

That should have caused its roof to collapse but miraculously it stayed upright, and looking through I could see Olympeon standing strong and proud in the southeast corner of the hill. But then my blood ran cold, for there on the upper floor, the floor devoted to the gods moved several giant figures in sombre fashion. The gateway to the heavens was open, other deities descending from the clouds into their home on earth, wandering round and waiting nonchalantly for decree to be made. For this was a summons, a call from one of the gods to hear judgement, upon a mortal.

Ingot and I stared in terror at each other before the golden head of the statue was ripped to pieces by its own hands. A face appeared beneath, a face that lived and breathed under its lifeless exterior. A war helmet covered her skull and forehead but her eyes moved beneath and she looked down at the red curtain and the hollow which held her box. Instinctively I moved towards my charge, the charge I was bound to protect for as long as I lived, but as I leant on my staff the huge cold eyes of this monster suddenly turned upon me and in a voice so terrible that even the gods in Olympeon stood still she yelled at me – "Get away from my box, Saman!"

8

Her face was twisted with rage and as I looked on she lifted her shield arm, smashing it on her own huge breastplate. Then she looked down at me and screamed aloud: "You Saman, you are guilty, and you will be punished." The gods in Olympeon cheered. "My lady," I beseeched her, "I beg you please of what crime am I guilty?" "Sacrilege," she roared, "and profanation. Do you hear, Saman? You have disobeyed my command and let mortal man see my treasures." "But the Abormine Oracle," I protested, "your own oracle told me I must let this young warrior lift its lid so that we might win the recent battle. Your oracle is your word, I obeyed only that." "No!" she screamed, "the only command you were to obey was my first command. Do not let any mortal man look in my box. Now you have betrayed me, now you will be punished." "Wait!" I cried getting to my feet. "I acted on your will. The oracle told me to let Ingot look inside and so I bid him do. You treat me unfairly."

It was a glance, a momentary glance towards Thrackan in Olympeon, but it was enough to tell me all that I needed to know. Thrackan belonged to the upper Council of Gods, the deities who spent their time making plans and devising the future of mankind, shaping and forming our destiny, and those gods had power and control over any oracle belonging to their fellow deities. "There is your betrayer!" I cried, "stand up to him, confront him and challenge him with the truth." It was useless. Thera could do nothing. Thrackan held sway over her and she would never challenge his authority. Instead she kicked downwards and blamed me once more for the rape of her treasure. "My judgement, Saman, is this – you will become the guardian of my box for all time. You will be immortal and you will stay here on Shadyridge until the end of the world itself, and as the years roll on unhappiness and misery will weigh heavier upon your shoulders, that your soul will weaken, your body grow tired, even as you consider each day your last, yearning for death as you contemplate your immortality and the perpetual state of your being. There is no end Saman for what you have done, only pain. Go now, and suffer. That is my decree and judgement. Justice has been done."

She lifted her huge spear in the air ready to bring the butt down hard upon the ground but I wasn't finished yet and in a loud voice that stopped her arm dead I shouted: "Justice!? It is just to punish he who sins, not he who is tricked by the sinner into sin. It is Thrackan, not I who should bear penalty. His is the crime, let him pay the price. You," I shouted turning in a fit of rage towards Olympeon to challenge the god of war himself, "you force me to shoulder the blame for this when you ordered it in the first place. That is not the work of a god, it is the work of a coward. I curse you now and all the gods for your deceit and betrayal. If I am to become immortal I will dedicate my unending days of misery and solitude to finding a way to undermine your authority and power." Continuing to glower at him feeling bold, defiant, unafraid, I barely noticed him pick the stone up from the floor beneath his feet.

"As for you," I said turning back to face our Earth-goddess, "revenge will be mine upon your head. I will grow far stronger than you, learning the ways of darkness and evil, and I will punish you as you punish me now, washing your memory clean with my spells and charms so that you will live mortal, without recollection of your godhead, and when you are so at a time when you least expect I will lure your friends and companions to your box and I will make them open it. When they do they will all perish. You have made me immortal - already power wells inside me coursing through my veins, strengthening my heart, hardening my soul. These things will come to pass. I will not fail. That is my final judgement and decree. Now justice has been done. Now you may bang your spear butt upon the ground."

But Thera could do nothing of the sort. She was too astounded by my gall. Her spear arm hung in the air, and as she continued to look down at me the I saw in her eyes something that I never thought I would ever behold in a deity - fear. Just a flicker, but that flicker made me feel more powerful than I had ever felt in my whole life. It wasn't the last time I would scare a god, not by any means. In fact as the years rolled past and centuries turned and as I studied and learned the powers that only immortals know fear in the eyes of a god by my doing became a commonplace of which I grew tired but at that moment when eternal life sat young upon my shoulders and when I first saw Thera scared by what I had said I felt bold and strong and a confidence I had never known before, an incredible surge of self-belief flowed through my body and swelled my pride to bursting point. I was immortal and omnipotent. Nothing could harm me, nothing.

But then I saw Thera's gaze shift once more towards the Olympeon and I realised I had overestimated my power. There stood Thrackan still looking on impassively and when Thera bowed her head he lifted his arm back and let the stone fly. I saw it coming, saw the stone cut through the air towards me but I didn't move quick enough and it slammed into my forehead with violent force. I heard the crack and then I blacked out.

9

When I came to I was on my own lying on the floor of the Bellanon. Ingot had gone, so had Thera and when I looked out towards Olympeon I saw that it was empty. The pathway to the heavens had closed. My head throbbed as I turned back to look at the statue beside me but only lumps and pieces of gold littered the ground where it had stood before. I dragged myself to my feet and made my way over to the red curtain that hid Thera's box from view. With one sweep of the hand I tore the curtain from its bindings and threw it away behind me, and there in the hollow beyond lay the box. I thought of all the days I had watched over it, wondering for a moment just exactly when I had become immortal but then I pushed that thought from my mind when I realised it was the concern of mortal man. What did I care about when I had become immortal, it was a question of time and the temporal meant nothing to me now. I was blessed with eternal life. I would live forever. For all time. Do you hear? I would outlive the young and the unborn and in a thousand years from now I would be no older than the man who stood at this moment looking thoughtfully at Thera's box.

Of course such thoughts filled me with excitement rather than fear in the early days of my immortality. I considered my condition to be a blessing instead of the curse that Thera intended it to be and I was full of hope for the future. But my immortality wasn't the same as those who die are granted nor the same as that enjoyed by the gods who live in perpetuity. That is an everlasting state of peace and tranquillity. This immortality tore me asunder and churned up my insides so that I was in constant state of turmoil. In ages to come I would watch the earth blossom and flower in the spring and my senses would be heightened. Joy would well up inside me and I would be glad beyond gladness that I had been granted eternal life. But then winter would come and darkness and decay would infect my soul with feelings of despair and hopelessness and I would curse Thera for forcing me to suffer so and worse each year when mortals barely noticed the change of seasons around them. Generations would come and go, civilisations would grow, flourish and die and I *would watch all this alone, friendless and I would wonder how Thera could have been so merciless as to inflict such suffering upon me when I had done nothing but guard her box and pay homage to her all my life.*

"Now however it was Ingot I cursed, Rathe's noble warrior who began to reap good and best fortune down in Rathe. I cared not that he followed my advice making weapons, building ships and designing defences to strengthen and fortify Rathe against invading armies, nor that he took credit himself for suggesting that we trade with our neighbours rather than fight wars against them. No, I didn't even care for his accruing riches from these enterprises that were rightfully mine. These things were not important to me because they were part of a world to which I no longer belonged. Rathe might be made stronger by the young warrior's hand, she might make a name for herself as a centre of trade and excellence but what did that matter when a hundred years from now she was likely to be conquered by an army stronger than her own that would subdue her and make her poor again? What did it matter that Ingot would grow rich when he would die and leave those riches behind? To him money was important, to me it was useless. What could wealth bring me that I did not have already? Immortality had stretched my sense of time. I now looked upon everything with an eye that used eternity to make its judgements whereas before when I was mortal I had used maybe a hundred years as a framework to judge the importance of these self-same things.

But, he still had to pay. In the days of his youth I had deemed him honourable, and when he had come to ask for my advice about what to do with his powers he had been humble and kindly, but the acquisition of power had corrupted his innocence and he had lost his integrity. As he grew older and more celebrated in Rathe so I learned more about the nature of immortality and most importantly about the nature of illusion. I fooled the warrior who had taken everything from me into thinking that he would be happy for evermore especially when he became old and lay on his death bed with his family around him. I had waited longingly for the moment and could hardly contain my excitement. There he was lying down telling my loved one that he could see the gods waiting to greet him in the next world and then he was dead, mine, and I flung him into perdition, the very annihilation of his soul.

Now, whenever I remember the look of fright on his face when he saw that it was me and not his precious gods who welcomed him into the next world, I always laugh long and hard. For the gods are weak and I am strong. They have punished me for a wrong I never committed and I will be revenged upon them all. Already I have mastered many powers and soon I will be able to undermine their authority in ways that they never dreamed possible. Then when this has been done I will make Thera human and I will fulfil my decree. I will lure the ones she loves, the ones she cares for most in the world to her own box and when they open the lid and consign themselves to annihilation I will be standing there, laughing. Some may think me cruel for what I plan. To them I say, "Thera started this, I shall end it. I am Saman, Chief Elder of Rathe, and I have spoken."

Roxie looks up from the small lamp, sure she notices movement.
She sees a Trustle.
The horns on its head twitch.
It claps its hands, bows and then shoots off.
Roxie knows only that she must follow.

10

The summit of Shadyridge.

Weather has deteriorated again.

Jack holds the box before him, gripping the clasp, stunned as it begins to undo itself.

He dives away as the lid opens sharply, expelling dirty brown light.

'Get back!' cries Mark, 'get away from it!'

'What's that noise?'

'It's the charge. The energy surge from the box.'

The swell bursts. punching them all off their feet.

Mark gropes around the floor, drawn to the box

He kneels before it, taking the prize in his hands.

Saman's cloak strokes the puddles beside him.

'Defy the gods.'

The clasp begins to undo itself again.

'Live blessed as Ingot.'

 Brilliant, dazzling light bursts from inside, the Earth-goddess herself flying out to land beside them.

She is wearing full body armour.

'Roxie! Why are you dressed like that?'

'It's a short story. Come on, I'll tell you.'

'Where's Saman.'

Jack holds the prize up, its sides now transparent.

'He's in the box. He's in the freaking box!'

Roxie slams the lid shut.

'Now we simply need a safe place to store him.'

11

The antique store in Rathe's parade.
Roxie carefully swaps boxes in the window.
As the Ratheans leave, they see townspeople pulling the Allhallows Festival banner down from its mooring.
'Well that's that for another year. Let's hope the next one's not as tempestuous.'
Thunder sounds.
Rain clouds form.
The four of them hightail it to the Tripsy Inn.

YOUNG SHAKESPEARE

1

A country of unbelief.
Its old order crumbling.
Tradition, civility, respect for authority no longer observed.
Faith, revelation, laughed from contention.
Observation, evidence forced upon a populace duped into
determinist belief so they lope round confused and dissatisfied, each
twisted narrative hammering another nail into their bled, drawn
hearts.
God abandoned.
Man as beast.
Evil rampant, its division overwhelming the populace.
This is England.
In the sixteenth century.

2

'William,' he'd snarl, 'where is William Shakespeare?'
I'd hide underneath the bed clothes, giggling. 'Not here. Next door.'
'Nonsense! You're cowering, boy. Come out!'
I'd peep from my hiding place and shrink beneath his mock-judicial
stare.
'No,' I'd cry, 'not predestination.'
'Oh yes, we have all been herded so.'
'But of free will. Don't we own choice?'
'None such exists. Only the elect are saved.'
He'd draw closer.
'You have been damned before your birth. How do you plead, sinner
of the skin?'
'Not guilty, father. Pride is ours to succumb to, else reject. My Lord
Saviour Jesus Christ protects me from its threat, and God's own
Love from the machinations of its prince.'
He'd straighten.
'Good. Now go and see its practice in the world.'

3

I was playing football.

I bumped into a pupil taking his last year, apologizing profusely to him because it was my first.

He studied me testily.

'Do you realise what you have just done, boy?

I shook my head.

'You have interrupted me in my thought.'

I sighed with relief.

'Which is the very worst thing you can do to a poet.'

'You're a writer!?'

He smiled.

'See that lad over there, the one being feted by his friends for every footballer's end goal?'

I nodded.

'Unpleasant he may be, but in fulfilling what the populace deems worthy he is lauded by them all. Will that be your wont, to earn approbation in such manner?'

'I don't know. I suppose so.'

'Fool! The common man's opinion counts for naught. Is that what you wish to be, a nobody?'

His manner softened.

'You are a pupil at King Edward VI School, William. Give over that public nuisance and spend time in study. You shall reap reward from it, that much is certain.'

'But I do study. I am keen with my education.'

'Let us test it then. Tell me of our dynasty.'

'Henry VII scored victory over Richard III at Bosworth Field.'

I glanced at him.

'Pretender threats from Lambert Simnel and Perkin Warbeck were overcome to establish the realm's unity, through fusing roses Lancastrian and York.'

'A good king then?'

'He kept the coffers full. Had Arthur lived, our country's direction would have proved straighter. As it is, the Mouldwarp married his wife, ditching her for Anne Boleyn whom he then beheaded for

Seymour. He sinned, sinned, and sinned again, each time with more severity. And in his position as monarch, took the country with him.'
'Explicate.'
'To annul his marriage with Catharine of Aragon he was driven to remove us from Rome's protection. Would that we had remained, for our leaving sweeps with it all sense of national identity.'
'Of Henry's many vices, which were most damaging?'
'Arrogance. Pride. Power. So has it always proved. Matilda against Stephen, Henry versus Becket, John at war with his nobles not to mention the mess he made in Ireland, whole countries riven for political and territorial gain, our own conquest by Vikings, Normans, the monarchical line still fighting for legitimacy now, because we have spurned the continent.'
'Of this break with Rome?'
'Henry opposed Luther before it benefited to befriend him. And Luther was misguided, misreading Augustine who misread Paul, who misread Jesus. And He embodied division most of all, bringing sword not peace to proceedings.'
He studied me closely.
'Talk to me about love. What do you know of it?'
'But little, I'm afraid.'
'Then learn. Such understanding ennobles a man. The best sort of love is holy. It has sanctity to it, defining and moulding the character, bringing it closer to God. It eases the burden of flesh, making whole our otherwise incomplete nature. Its experience will also make you a great writer.'
I baulked.
'But I'm going to be an actor. It is all the rage at present.'
'Pretender? What use is that? This country needs more writers, not fakers. You have the gift, Master Shakespeare, it would be a shame to waste it learning lines when you could be composing them.'
'But I've never given it a moment's thought. Why do you advise me so?'
'Not I, the Headmaster. He thinks you're quite some Chaucer.'
And chuckling so, he strolled off across the field, right through the middle of the football match.

4

Predestination.

A notion heretical for those who strove to justify themselves through good works.

Free will was God's gift, we believed, making it our choice to be saved or damned irreparably by how we conducted ourselves in this life.

Act nobly, with love for fellow man and the common weal, or exist as beasts, preying on others for our benefit and self-advancement.

Salvation.

Damnation.

The choice was ours.

Our free will.

Gifted to us, by God.

But then poison had seeped into the system.

As I'd said to Richard at school, misreading.

My own included.

For in my subsequent study of scripture, I realized how in error I had been to attribute discord to Jesus, knowing now his sword was by metaphor the living and active word of God and that his simple message was for us to repent and turn face to the Father.

That to save, not judge nor condemn the world was His purpose.

But that teaching had been twisted quite out of shape by the reformers who gave us now a God deciding not only before our births which of us merited salvation but also which of us would be damned once we died.

His judgment.

Made upon us.

Before we were even born.

Double predestination, it was termed, and it stank.

Because it was unjust.

For how many of us fell in the sins of youth to be recovered, saved by grace of the Almighty, who loved, not hated the world, wishing only for us to live by truth in it so that we might better resist its manifold traps and temptations?

My peer, Richard Field, was righteous, a good man so it turned who went on to lead honourable life in honourable profession, as a printer.

Then there was my own father, John, who committed illegality in his trade, who made questionable then immoral choices but who aware enough to see the error of his ways was repentant, turning his effort in action from dubious dealing to sober undertaking.

Heaven rejoiced many more times over his salvation than Richard's, because the latter already trod the path of love, my father moving from the nettles of hate thereunto.

You see, the problem with predestination was its mercilessness. It had none, and it gave none.

It was a concept embodying malice aforethought, and I loathed it. Yet for all that, the dreadful idea stuck in my mind because of the inevitable misfortune we all experienced in life.

If God was the God of love, why did He make us suffer?

Why, in particular, did He permit evil to flourish so that it wrecked people's already precarious state of existence?

Why not extirpate the very loathsome figure who seemed to personify its cruelty, Lady Fortune?

After Richard had told me our Headmaster thought I was some present day Chaucer, I had quite put the comment to the back of my mind, but one overcast afternoon in the depths of winter I found myself returning to a place I hadn't frequented for as long as I could remember, the book shop on the corner of the street where I lived. Chaucer I had been labelled, and so I responded, reading all I could about this poet before tackling the works themselves, his translation of a piece by the Roman writer Boethius catching and then enveloping my imagination profoundly.

The Consolation of Philosophy was written whilst Boethius served time in prison, unjustly and adversely accused. He had fallen from high standing to imminent demise in the form of his own execution so for him the concept of Fortune's wheel upon which in her caprice she spun us all was logical and real, because its reality had quite overtaken and possessed his situation itself

> *Swich is my strengthe and this pley I pleye continuely. I torne the whirlynge wheel with the turnynge sercle; I am glad to chaungen the loweste to the heyeste, and the heyeste to the lowest.*

Note the tone.

Not just the wickedness, but the delight in causing misery to others, climactically so for her when she herself had been the cause of their undoing.

As the school year progressed, Richard had introduced me to further material, most notably the Arthurian legends and I had devoured as much reading matter upon the subject as I could.

Legend or not, these were tales that centred on love, they were about a king who ruled with love, except they culminated in one of the most notorious betrayals of all, the affair of Arthur's wife Guinevere with his most trusted friend, Sir Lancelot.

And this seemed to be the case with each story I encountered.

There was a reversal of fortune.

If the characters were lucky, they were returned to the status with which they had started the tale, but in the majority of cases Fortune's wheel spun only once, not just leaving them at bottom, but with their friends, or more often their enemies at top.

What kind of world was this, I began to question, in which evil people succeeded, not just in and amongst themselves but at the very expense of the good, the noble, the honest and just?

There was only one answer, I feared, my spirit depressed greatly as I came to realization that God had simply forsaken us, leaving the world behind to fend for itself.

5

'Talk to me about love. What do you know of it?'
I woke with a start, the fire-breathing hound receding from my mind as the dream dissolved.
Rising from bed, I walked the short distance from my room to my father's.
It was still dark, though severing streaks of light were beginning to threaten the night sky, a sliver of moon sending grimy light down upon his face which seemed contorted, though it was his body position that startled me, hands in prayer, legs crossed tightly and pulled right up to his chest.
His eyes suddenly shot open and he grabbed hold of my arm.
'Do you fear God?'
I struggled to free myself.
'Do you, though?'
'Dad,' I said desperately, 'wake up.'
'But there is so much hatred in the world.'
He sank back, then woke properly.
'You have new work to look forward to. A new life. In fresh location.'
'What on earth…'
He fell asleep again.
And I simply could not rouse him.

6

The theatre was tiny.

The back room minute.

Barely enough space for me, let alone the apprentice who joined my project work not several days after I had begun employment there.

I introduced Anne to the play which copy I was currently making, a piece whose protagonist was vocal in his disregard for the dead and departed from this sphere.

'He's a fool,' she said after a while at her transcription.

'Who is?'

'This writer.'

I shifted position.

'I think we're supposed to be copying, not commenting.'

'Do you think he's a fool though, like I do?'

I remained silent.

'You must have an opinion, William.'

'It is not form to discuss the work whilst we make copy of it.'

'Don't you even consider it?'

'Yes,' I fulminated, 'I do. He's a reformer, and I'm a believer in tradition. He doesn't have faith in the things I do, so we must head our separate ways.'

She studied me.

'You're far more alike than you care to think. His beliefs may subvert your credence, but your own undermine his progression with every day that passes.'

'What do you mean?'

'We are all the same,' she cried suddenly, 'proceeding from one source, branching into millions of tributaries which then collect in one mouth. The sea binds us all, and in turn is bound by its creator, Love.'

'Love doesn't rule the world,' I choked, 'there is hate everywhere.'

'You speak only of your own soul.'

'Good intentions go athwart,' I cried myself, 'benevolence is met with rancour, warmth with disregard, and well meant words with ridicule. The place is horrible, yet people like you believe it a land in which virtue should be practiced.'

'I said nothing of virtue, though that quality is its own reward, regardless of whether or not the world acquieces.'

'I have studied, Anne, I know nature of this cosmos we inhabit. Fortune spins her wheel, and all of us who once ride the crest of its benevolence will eventually suffer the turpitude of her misanthropy.'

She sighed.

'Your world summation sounds like the ill-considered conclusion of all dualist heretics. Zoroaster, Mani, the Cathars, Bogomils, what propagation have they been afforded by ignoring the wise instruction of Holy Spirit?'

She leant in close.

'Look at me. Look into my eyes, look, we carry Truth down the ages, women, but we require men to express it. It is trapped within us, and men like you must exorcise it onto the page.'

She was inches from my face now, on a sudden leaning forward to kiss me full on the lips, my soul springing up through my body and eyes, twining itself with her own in relish of such vital, fresh bond.

And then she was gone, pulled away and from the room abruptly.

I was too stunned to follow.

By the time I did, she was nowhere to be seen.

I looked round.

The theatre was deserted.

Eerie in its darkness, its silence and stillness quite at odds with the vibrancy performance always brought to the place.

My gaze was drawn to the trap door in middle of the stage though I moved not towards it for feeling sudden fatigue.

I fought hard against it, but the sense became overwhelming.

I heard voice, loud and assured

A closet, and a Popish wag!

Shaking my head and rubbing my eyes against the tiredness, the same impertinence sounded in my ears

A dirty doubter from Douai!

I took to rest.

And rest became sleep.

I saw Anne floating towards me, her arms outstretched, her face beaming with delight.

I reached out to embrace her, to taste once more the fecundity of her lips, and as we kissed I began to feel the imparting profundity of her spirit, the secret wisdom of its gender proffering teachings from epochs and aeons before mine own.

I saw Chaucer reading Boethius, Alfred the Great also and my own Queen Elizabeth surveying his work before I was catapaulted into my own future where I sat composing my tragic masterpiece.

My masterpiece?

Ha!

A foul effluent from the poisoned swamp of my mind, my magnum opus in which I plumbed the very depths of my own dejection to pluck pitiful characters and parade them in gross, distorted gyves before the populace.

Suddenly I came to, Anne before me.

'Psychomachia,' she whispered. 'The fight for our souls, William, between the forces of good and evil. We have been granted speech in this regard, and it alone saves or condemns us.

She moved towards me.

'We need you to heal division, so reconcile antitheses. The imagination is the faculty through which truth is revealed. Listen carefully, and you will hear it speak to you. You, William, have the strongest imagination of all.'

As though in confirmation, I somehow pictured scene following of which she spoke.

'John Dee instigated literary circle at Mortlake some years ago, but the writers assembled had not strong enough skill to bind spiritual and material realms together. Further group has been established at Wilton, led ably by Sir Philip Sidney's sister. They have taken over the mantle, yet struggle still to solve a problem which grows larger by the day.'

She moved towards the trap door.

'God is leaving the universe behind, and we must stop Him. What if I was to tell you that beneath this stage lies the entrance to another world?'

'I would think you were mad.'

There is a secret passage beneath here, and we will take it momentarily.'

'Why?'

'Because Sir Walter Raleigh would first speak with you at Durham House, and from there you and I must travel many miles west, to Salisbury Cathedral.'

I laughed.

'It is over one hundred and fifty miles from here to Salisbury. Who on earth would build such a tunnel?'

She drew closer.

'The wisdom had to be made secure. I say again, your imagination is fervent beyond belief, and truth seeks to speak through it. But truth is not the only force that would like to possess you.'

My face dropped.

'Fear not. The Supreme pushes you down this path, but He does not take His hand from your flank.'

'And what if I decide not to comply?'

'You will simply delay the inevitable. Time is cyclical, it opens and shuts accordingly. What is postponed now will be fulfilled later. Thought is a vent, William, which opens and closes breathing upon successive ages the pure, clear wisdom of the universe. But it is an implement deceptive, for in turning the soil of our minds it replaces muddy memory with lush recollection.'

And then she was off, crouched down and disappeared from view.

I stared after her, the inky dark seeming to stretch away forever so that I drew back in wariness, but then I gathered myself, clambering quickly away from the upper stage into the passage below.

7

The initial surface on which I crawled suddenly fell away so that I landed with a thud beneath.

I glanced up at the trap door, but my attention was drawn ahead to the passage, lit at intervals by the flames of torches hanging from brackets in the walls, shelves running along their length filled with dusty manuscripts.

For a moment I stared in awe, and then I picked one at random opening it carelessly to have my sight and sound battered

I AM THAT I AM

I reeled back, knocking into the shelf on the other side from which further manuscript fell onto me, springing open to sound the same declaratory words

I AM THAT I AM

The truth repeated itself not only on the vellum and through the air but in my mind also, as though what I saw on the parchment and heard from it resonated with something I already knew within me.

I closed and opened the book at different place, but the same words were written therein making the same sounds therefrom, and again when I thumbed to a new part, and again when I replaced the second folio and reopened the first, the same words blazing trail from the page through the air into my heart

I AM THAT I AM

Suddenly I was beset by notional opposites - revenge, mercy, sanity and madness, action, delay, all jostling angrily in my mind for priority topped by the ultimate antithesis which had so troubled my consciousness for years, only this time the two concepts predestation and free will were utterly reconciled.

I completed puzzle with my mother.

It was winter but we were snug inside, and I felt safe, engaged with a
task whose wholesome endeavour the two of us shared accordingly.
The challenge was a difficult one, its final picture eluding me.
I moved a piece.
My mother added one.
I pushed another into place.
She compensated for that with a further.
Before I knew it we had finished, sitting back with satisfaction,
though the picture which stared up at us from the floor was one of
the most disturbing I had ever laid eyes upon.
There was a storm, for gnarled and knotted trees bent back in its
gale, clinging to the sides of a brown hillock whose mottled brush
overlay stones of varying magnitude, themselves wedged awkwardly
into this mound and topped by two more trunks disappearing into the
coal-black skies above.
Amongst this inhospitable bracken sat two figures – the first dressed
in flowing robes of state, pushed over and away from his under tunic
by the same torrent against which he railed in desperation, his hands
aloft as though manacled to the air which so exasperated him, his
beard and hair blown coarse, his eyes rigid and unbelieving, the hilt
of his senseless sword just visible at his belt, silly red garters tucked
into a pair of cream, ill-suited shoes for this inclemency in which he
pleaded for himself, uselessly.
There lay, facing him, a creature of the most inexact proportion,
great lengthy pointed shoes held by gaudy baubles, a brown linen
tunic skirted by yet more bells on his belt and the obscenely pointed
hood of his clown's hat foisted down the back of his jerkin, its gaudy
orange only lessened by the revolting red and white striped upper
garment which ended at his hands holding up his jutting jaw, bloated
mouth, death-scythed eyes, frowning eyebrows and tonsured pate –
what a revolting parody of a man, and that in childish pose as though
watching some deliciously light enterprise before him.
And then the image was no more, and I was staring at the open
manuscript before me, blank now, wholly and quite without
statement of attribution divine.
I kicked the book to one side and ran, pelting down the narrow
passage, the flames from the torchlights swishing and crackling in
their brackets over, after me, other noise behind, turning my
attention to see the passageway empty.

It was running water I heard, its dull eternal flow connecting sharply with my imagination as though it somehow lay within my head.

For a moment then, the natural world merged with my soul, and just as suddenly it departed, but the vivid and intense moment would remain in my memory long after the event.

In fact, it would inform my entire future output.

Right then, there, birth and death met in obloquy of time contracted, squeezed, stretched then nascent through my ears.

I thought I saw my own parents standing at the altar of love bedecked in finery, glowing, joyful, younger than I ever knew them, but then they turned towards me their faces drained of happiness, tired, drawn, wan, as the waxing moon's shadow fell dim across contours of their once sunny faces.

They merged.

The image collapsed.

And suddenly booming all around me so loud I had to cover up my ears against its noise

KNOW THYSELF!

I sank down on my haunches.

KNOW THYSELF!

I lay prostrate on the floor.

KNOW THYSELF!

I curled up in the foetal position.

KNOW THYSELF!

I heard other sound, looking up to see clods of earth cascading down towards me.

I flung my arms above my head to protect myself, braced wildly for the crush, but there was none and when I dared to look again I was back in the tunnel, alone, staring down its rigid, mildewed length.

Suddenly, something hit me.

I reached down to pick up a small stone.

KNOW THYSELF!

Dear God, the inanimate held voice.

I dropped it on the instant, then leant to pick it up again.

This time it remained silent.

The stone remained quiet!

And then blood began to seep through my fingers.

At first, I thought it was my own, that some sharp edge had pierced my hand with this result, but when I took it in my other paw I realised it was the rock itself which weeped.

KNOW THYSELF!

The words punched me back up into the tunnel.

The tunnel in which I already stood.

I was back in the tunnel.

KNOW THYSELF!

Behind me.

KNOW THYSELF!

In front.

KNOW THYSELF!

To each side.

KNOW THYSELF!

Above.

Good grief, light streamed down upon me.

And, reassuringly, a smiling face looked on my travail.

Hands extended towards me.

I reached up without question, was grasped.

And there I found myself in comforting surroundings, a home, a castle, refuge come quite upon me at exact moment I thought insanity had squashed all normalcy from the confines of my mind.

I had reached the end of this particular line.

I was back in civilization.

In the real world.

Well, at Durham House anyway.

8

'Thank God,' I mouthed as he hauled me into the chamber, 'thank you.'

My relief was tempered as without word he marched me towards the door and onto a sizeable courtyard bordered by apartments and a gatehouse in the south east corner.

Soon, we had entered another complex and in a moment we found ourselves in the property's chapel, my companion pushing me through the pews and up into the choir stalls before turning to stairs leading back downwards.

As we made to descend, I looked up to see a large wooden cross before the gathering gloom and dusk of the underground brought recollection of the tunnel to my mind, whereupon I struggled violently to loose myself.

'Whoa there!' cried the chamberlain, 'whatever's the matter, young lad?'

'I'm not going down there.'

'Come, come, it owns means of escape.'

He smiled.

'There are secret rooms enough in this residence reached by the fireplace and through the bookcase, some accessed by locking devices, others through hidden mechanisms. There are trapdoors beneath rugs, like the one from which you emerged just now, watertight arches that link exterior chimneys to underground rivers, and deep wells which lead to caves behind waterfalls.'

He put his hand around my shoulder again, and gently led me further into the crypt.

'Come now,' he said as I faltered down the steps, 'the seabirds travel from the Mediterranean Sea to the Atlantic Ocean.'

I frowned.

'They soar through the Pillars of Hercules on their way outward, and flap back through the Strait on their way inward.'

He descended further.

'The water travels both ways also. The denser below, and westward, the less heavy above, eastward.'

Still further down we went.

'The human swell, back and forth across the Strait, physically, culturally, remained unspoilt for centuries. Then it was ruptured, grew distinct, and at last separated.'

He fiddled about in the gloom, pulling on a lever.

Murky light crawled into the crypt.

I looked to see a small, decrepit staircase winding its way back upwards and then he led on, climbing the creaking, rickety steps for a short while until we reached a door at the top, which he flung open in the most dramatic fashion.

Suddenly we were in a new room, and this quite the most welcoming and well furnished little space in which I had ever stepped foot. It was circular too, leading me to surmise that we were in one of Durham House's turrets.

'In the daytime,' said my guide, 'you may see the Thames from this window. Beyond that, well Westminster, Whitehall Palace, the Surrey Hills...'

He tailed off in boredom.

'Come on now, mind out Kit.'

I looked down expecting to see him clearing a cat off the furniture but was instead utterly taken aback by the sight of a figure seemingly entwined in the embroidery of one of the many colourful chairs before me.

But my surprise was quickly dispersed by the ongoing and seemingly inexhaustible recitation this fellow seemed intent on delivering to me.

'The Ancient Greeks,' he breezed, 'thought St Michael's Cave was the entrance to the Underworld. They believed that the very Gates of Hades lay within its maw. Much deception came of this, none more misleading and fraudulent than Plato's assertion that the city of Atlantis lay beyond the Straits which this make believe tunnel was meant to bridge.'

He leant in towards me.

'See how falsehood feeds on itself so that deception grows greater and more profound as its belly fattens.'

He gestured to a rolled up parchment on the desk beside me.

'There is a land which lies beyond the Strait and it is one of far greater import than that of misty, shifty Atlantis.'

He unravelled the paper to reveal a map on which a great landmass stretched from the top of Europe to the bottom of Africa and lower, except it was on the other side of the western ocean.

'This,' he said proudly 'is America. The Queen herself wishes for me to make an empire of it for the Crown. Not for me the barbarity and slaughter of Ireland, no Spenser can have Munster, and make of her what fairy he wishes. I will dally here, I and Oxford, flatulent Oxford, who nonetheless spins rather a decent turn with his quill.'

'So you are Raleigh. Sir Walter Raleigh.'

Suddenly someone entered.

'Attend,' cried Raleigh maniacally at me, 'for without understanding we are as useless as the base fabric spun by that harpy on her handrail.'

His eyes flashed with eminent madness.

'Hold the world in contempt, my dear fellow, wonder not why it fails to fulfil your decree but instead align yourself with its futile and fetid proroguing. Love philosophy, loathe everyday wisdom, fly from the vanity of fools and marvel not at their illusions of adequacy. Lose yourself in poetry, savour its delight, promote its virtue, for it is the very belly of mankind from which veins and their vestibules stud and suffuse the body politic. Make by imitation, strive to cultivate power to move your audience – a metaphor that teaches is a picture which speaks, in instruction removed from its origin, in fulfilment greater than first construct. The man who suffers to extremity is the man who may utterly express himself, free from personality, absorbed by sacrifice, unspoiled, harmonious, in pastoral Arcadia where Arcas, Pan and Virgil dine together in *memento mori*. And you must join them. Respect your forebears, but fear your precursors. Always.'

He turned to Kit.

'Please, continue whilst Harriot and I convene.'

With rapidity of motion, he took his companion from the room whereupon Kit emerged from the furniture and took us both to the window out of which we looked upon the darkness outside.

For long minutes we stood in silence, but I felt comfort not disease in his company.

He had not the frenzy of Raleigh, only calm surety which drew me to him.

'Tell me, William, what do you see?'

'But little. It is night time.'

'Look more closely. What now?'

'Pinpricks of light in the sky. Stars.'

'And what would you see from this window, in the daylight?'

'The Thames, and beyond that, well Westminster, Whitehall Palace, the Surrey Hills. Of what use is this exercise?'

He leant towards me.

'Raleigh will tarry with language but he has not the strong poet's vision. The night is man's conception, that is why he looks outward to the heavens, for answer. Of course, he finds nothing there but discord, confusion, what our host terms harpy, when in fact Lady Providence holds sway over it all, cutting shapes from the night and trickling them through her fingertips so they fall as shafts of light upon us. She is light, William, the light of Love, and in the brightness of her day you may see not only the Thames, Westminster, Whitehall Palace, and the Surrey Hills, but the whole globe beyond.'

He paused.

'Yet under the pressure of paternity her sheen is smudged, his dark cognizance seeing alone competitors to be bested and enemies fought in order to claim the spoils of futile campaigns.

He moved towards a small weaving loom I had not noticed before.

'Come,' he said running his fingers along the top of it, 'talk to me of this spindle.'

'There is a hook at the top of the shaft,' I said, 'and a whorl at the other end. The hook spins the shaft, which in turn rotates the whorl.'

'Who works it?'

'Bess, I should think.'

'The woman is Fortune,' he scowled, 'who wove all the world into being on her loom, measuring, twining everyone together before severing with glee the threaded whirligig upon which we rotate incessantly. I grow tired of Durham House,' he said moving forward, 'it is not the place of which I was promised so much. Atomism needs for it no reason, no purpose, it is mechanistic only. Once, I was satisfied with such fare. Now, it leaves me cold.'

He advanced further.

'Scholasticism is on the wane, my dear fellow, Aristotelian conception fading, replaced even now by fresh system of logic.'

Suddenly, and from whence I knew not, he produced quite the most pulchritudinous plant I had ever seen.

I gawped at the specimen, bowled over by its beauty, its pungent aroma filling my nostrils 'Where did you get that?'

'It is powerful,' he grinned manically, 'is it not? For you ask me alone from whence I obtained the object, not concerning the manner in which I have managed to conceal such largesse since you entered the room.'

He put the plant down on one side and drew from another bottomless pocket of his some kind of tube with a piece of glass at both ends. 'This,' he said noting my interest, 'is a telescope. It allows the viewer at one moment,' and here he applied the object to his right eye, 'to see a great distance away, miles, leagues even with the correct adjustment.' He took it from his eye. 'That is how Raleigh views matter. But,' and here he spun the telescope round before affixing it to his other eye, 'this is how you see the world, in detail minute, not proudly swelling.'

He put the telescope down and rifled in his pockets once more. 'This is tobacco,' he grinned keenly, 'and you ingest it with one of these.' He held a small tube with shallow receptacle at one end.

'It is a pipe,' he continued, stuffing the cup with tobacco, 'though once you light the end, you do not blow out, but suck inwards, taking puffs, like this.'

He passed it straight to me.

I put the pipe to my mouth and inhaled deeply, feeling a terrible rasp in my throat, through my nostrils, down my gullet and out of my nose.

I coughed viciously, holding the object at arm's length.

'Exhale less,' he said, 'inhale more.'

I put the pipe to my mouth again and drew breath once more, in gentler fashion. It worked, and I enjoyed the first sensation of tobacco coursing through the veins of my body, a deeper sense of peace as the drug snaked about, coiled round and then fanged right through my lungs.

I looked at Kit, but he had vanished.

Dumbly, I searched the embroidered furniture, sight suddenly hazy as my surroundings seemed to cave in upon themselves, gobbling, swallowing everything from tobacco to telescope, chairs, window, the very night outside, voices sounding from the plangent stars, a conversation between untold number, the ghosts of every person who had lived since the world began, concerted whisper of millions, nay billions of souls departed from this sphere

The Spinner of Fate twines good and bad together

Spirits floated around me

My loom stands still, the wool drops from my hands

I began to panic

Man lives by chance, to Fate subdued...
And evil thrives, for Fate is blind

Yet God suffered from no such deficiency, I knew that.
He cared for my folk, for me, our lives, our safety, our country.
But then the terrible thought, that dreadful idea began to surface
again.
Where had He been, I thought, when the reformers had ransacked
our churches, made firewood from the altars, burnt the hymnals and
torched the very crosses we held so absolutely dear as sign of our
Saviour's ransom?
Why had He allowed them to rut through our sacred buildings
shoving aside the poor and needy, destroying the relationship these
vulnerable folk had with the church by slashing the tie which bound
them in dependence upon the church for alms and other sustenance?
The fowl who kept the rafters in our beautiful, unspoilt chapels must
have wagged their feathers in dismay at the venality and hypocrisy
of a king who had the effrontery to maintain he was a religious man
whilst he was heaping misery on his own populace by redistributing
pilfered finances to the Crown.
For that was what bit, the greed.
They said Henry showed consideration in his actions, but my parents
never saw any evidence to justify that assertion, only the
displacement of ordinary people who had relied on the church their
whole lives, and the pressure, the constant pressure applied by the
reformers for them to accept, conform or simply ignore what was
happening to our heritage, our traditions, the very soul of our
country.
I also heard that Henry was unaware of the full impact of his policy
of Dissolution.

That was a lie.

Well might he go about continuing to perform his daily Masses but in my opinion Defender of the Faith sat on his shoulders no more easily than the gout in his feet and the folds of blubber which prevented him from standing up on his infected limbs.

He was concupiscent, and his legacy was, and will always be, this – that for lust, and lust alone, he broke with Rome, and that for avarice he tore the churches and monasteries from our land to fill the empty coffers of his kingship.

God had nothing to do with the Dissolution.

It was conducted by human hands

And the king's were bloodiest of all.

He hadn't just wiped out the monasteries, he had by consequence of the pillage, started the process of disintegrating our very society.

We lived for community.

Serving each other, and the monarchy, wasn't just an expectation, it was an integral and sustaining part of our identity, as inhabitants of the land, citizens of the country, united, practising one and the same faith.

We saw to one another's needs because it was the right, proper, decent, and Christian manner so to uphold – altruism, or charity, was a cornerstone of the church's teaching; in serving one another, and in obedience to authority, to hierarchy, our selves grew centred, enabling us to see with the inner vision of truth.

As Anne had intimated, the simplest way to tell whether or not somebody abided by such truth was through listening to how they spoke.

Good men talked well of one another, bad men ill.

Which ineluctably transported to action.

For this was the sort of behaviour you began to see in people once the country started to reel from the damage inflicted upon it – to tell the truth became shameful, as mendacity twisted morality so that those who sought to maintain the distinction between right and wrong were jeered at by the fools who had without thought smudged the two colours in palette of their own spineless conception.

It was said by those who clung to the old faith that before the break from Rome society was strong, ordered, united, but that with the division wrought by Henry's carnage everyday life grew confusing, that uncertainty and fear became the prevailing factors, and reality for the populace became a murky half-light of false semblance, as though some parasite had wormed its way into our host body politic, the commonweal, and sat there, masquerading peacefully as us whilst it feasted greedily upon our innards.

Again, the test was simple – in a false community, good men and women were ignored, or in more sinister fashion, silenced, and that often by vainglorious folk who had nothing to offer anyone but vacuity and falsehood.

After all, this is what happened in a broken society.

People like this came to the fore.

If we all served community, such folk receded.

They were purged, by the very selfless and noble actions wrought to aid society.

Take Envy.

Its source could be as simple as feeling discomfort at the good fortune of others so that the country's ordinary citizens already jammed behind boulders in the rapids were then shot at with arrows by Henry and his henchmen, unable to protect themselves not just from Fortune's Wheel but from the gleeful thugs who'd stuck rocks in its cogs so that it stopped, or so it felt like to us, with the fraudulent riding crest of a foul, gluttonous wave whilst the gentle were churned over in its grim, muddy wash beneath.

A close knit community could withstand the buffets of everyday life. One divided had no chance but to roll punch drunk with every slap, hit, punch and kick that was aimed at it, and that more often than not from a Europe only too keen to have England back in the fold, eagerly licking its chops at the thought of using a willing Scotland or Ireland for a standpoint from which to launch an attack into the mainland.

It was said maternal love might also keep a society welded together, that the warmth and constancy of its women more often than not ensured that a community remained whole.

What acidic precept had the nation's womenfolk been scorched by on that accord!

Mary and Elizabeth may have shared common ground through suffering persecution in their youth but they were entirely polarised when it came to deciding the country's faith.

Our present queen, Elizabeth, modelled herself on Marguerite, Queen of Navarre and why not for her exemplary behaviour, generosity of spirit and erudition were certainly the qualities to stoke admiration in the heart of a young, impressionable Princess? Marguerite was Socratic in outlook, owning humility enough not just to tolerate her opposition but to befriend them and thus display the charity exemplified by Jesus, her faith a dialectic debate in which seemingly opposing beliefs sought to resolve their apparent differences rather than establish their own version of Christianity as the correct, God-given creed.

Except Marguerite was Queen of Navarre.

Not France.

She was Queen of a kingdom.

Not a country.

For colonies, as Sir Walter would soon find out, cause issues.

Kingdoms, as Aethelstan, Edmund and Eadred in our own land knew, cause problems.

But countries, well, countries were an entirely different matter altogether, vast and intractable slabs of land with vast and intractable and quite irresolvable conflicts of interest, whether they be between individuals, families, factions or whole sectors of the populace.

Take England.

Tudor England.

Elizabeth was, of course, at the very heart of brutal and often merciless policy, but after the destruction of both her brother Edward and her sister Mary's reigns, she was determined herself to tread the *via media*, to bring stability and longevity to an increasingly dislocated and fragmented society.

Yet her religious settlement but hostile to one side, had not reached far enough in its reform by opinion of the other. She thus found herself in the unenviable position of having alienated both her opponents and members of her own sorority.

She couldn't win, she could not win.

But what if I could?

What if I wrote, and in composition fused necessary antitheses together, that the words I put to paper might somehow reconcile my country's divisions?

And for that I would head for Salisbury, as Anne had advised, to offer services to this group at Wilton so to help in halting God's departure from our sphere.

I swallowed.

I would have to traverse the tunnel again, to make passage thither. To travel above ground, my sense resisted.

I left the room, retracing my steps down stairs and then back up and through the chapel, expecting at any moment to meet Raleigh and Harriot, but I never did see them, only noticing once more the wooden cross as I made my way across the courtyard and back into the room I had first entered Durham House.

I hesitated, then pulled the carpet back to reveal trap door beneath. I paused again, fearful of what words this time might bash into my ears and eyes.

I took last look at my surroundings, then ducked into the tunnel beneath…

TO BE CONTINUED

Printed in Great Britain
by Amazon